THE UPSIDE OF DEATH

Parker Rimes

CONTENTS

CHAPTER 1

The best thing about a spirit guide is he warns you when your future turns ugly. The worst? Sometimes he doesn't. Keera remembered that the moment the front door opened by itself.

A large man grabbed her hand—keys still in it—and yanked her inside like a paper doll.

"Welcome home," he said, his accent thick and slurry. Eastern European.

Russian, maybe. His pale blue eyes drilled into hers with a carnal gleam. An animal. He kicked the door shut and dragged her into the living room. Her heart thumped, frantic enough to fracture a rib.

Two other men waited there, dressed like him—jeans, black leather.

"Miss Keera Miles," one said. Shoulder-length black hair, about her height.

The Animal dropped her hand. Longhair took it, kissed it. Old-world courtesy, fake as a plastic tiara. His hand was fleshy and limp.

Keera stayed silent. Her mind spun when it needed to stay sharp. Who are these people? she asked Bardo silently. What do they want?

They want you. You're valuable to them, her spirit guide replied, his tone almost scolding. She should have stayed alert. Should have used her instincts.

A third man stood by the window. Blond, thin, watchful. He said nothing. His eyes slipped away from contact.

Keera turned back to the Animal—over two hundred pounds, most of it upper body, and no hair in sight. He stood a clenched fist over six feet. She knew instantly—he was the danger. It came to her like a radio signal: clear and loud.

She scanned the room slowly, pretending calm she didn't feel. She wasn't scared. She was petrified.

The men had made themselves comfortable. Three carry-on bags on the floor. Scuff marks on the mahogany coffee table. Two bottles of Stolichnaya vodka on the mantel. Her shot glasses—souvenirs from a long-ago Russian field trip—were now in full use.

"Please," said Longhair, touching her arm and gesturing to the couch.

The Animal moved to the mantel and unscrewed a bottle. The tinny splash of vodka added a new fear: they were drinking on the job. She lowered her handbag and briefcase by her feet and sat.

"Allow me to introduce ourselves," Longhair said. "We're your caregivers for the next few days." His voice gravelly, his manner unhurried.

She took in every detail, filing it away for the police—if there was a later. Right now, her instincts had shut down.

The blond man downed a shot in one gulp.

The Animal's gaze raked over her before settling on her chest. She folded her arms, then thought better of it and clasped her hands in her lap. Thank God she'd worn a denim jacket over her summer dress.

"How did you get in here?" Her voice came out squeaky. "I'm calling the police if you don't leave."

"You won't call anyone," Longhair said.

"How did you open the locks? Who are you, and what do you want?"

"Locks? Household locks?" He shrugged. "What man can make, man can unmake."

"Are you Russian mafia? I don't run a business. I have no profits to skim. I'm a lecturer in anthropology. You've got the wrong person."

He smiled—unbothered, amused.

"Mafia is an Italian word, a great Russian once said. Does it matter what we are? You're coming with us. We'll be your constant companions for a while."

You are valuable to them, Bardo had said. It had passed over her then. Now it slammed into place like a trap.

"You're kidnapping me?" No. Impossible. That wasn't her life. This was madness, some elaborate prank. Except it wasn't, it was real. And Bardo had confirmed it.

She was supposed to meet Zach. If she didn't call him, he'd come by—too late. Her psychic sense was all static now, but one message came through clearly: they were leaving. Soon.

"Kidnap?" Longhair said. "More of a compulsory home stay with new friends. May I have your bag

"You're robbing me first?"

"We don't deal in bags. I need your ID. Mistakes are common in this line of work."

"You're insane. The Department of Anthropology won't pay ransom for a junior staff member."

"We're not asking them. Your bag, please."

She started to open it, but he took it, flipped open the flap, turned it over, and dumped the contents on the coffee table.

"You bastard." Rage surged at the violation.

The Animal set down his glass and stepped toward her, but Longhair raised a hand.

"Ostav'ee," he said in Russian.

Keera's Russian was basic, but she understood. *Leave her.* The Animal hesitated, then returned to his drink.

Longhair turned back to her. "You're in no position to speak rudely."

He sifted through the mess—receipts, business cards, lipstick, moisturizer, tissues, phone, some coins, and her father's old wallet. He switched off the phone and pocketed it. Then emptied the wallet. Credit cards. A hundred dollars. Driver's license. More business cards. He picked up the license and compared the photo to her face.

"You photograph beautifully," he said. "Such an excellent likeness." He drained his vodka. "When this is over, I can offer you a modeling job. No dancing required. Very good money."

She said nothing.

Longhair's leather jacket creaked as he reached for her satchel. He pulled out notepads, student assignments, and a voice recorder. Pink Post-Its fluttered off the folders.

"You should be more organized," he muttered.

He glanced at the blond man, who walked across the room and picked up a long green canvas bag from near the bay windows. She hadn't noticed it until now. The late sunlight caught it perfectly. It was long enough to fit a large child.

Or her.

Longhair stood. The Animal moved behind her. She heard the bottle cap again—another round of drinks?

No. A glass was shoved at her.

"Drink," the Animal said.

Keera shook her head. He gripped it in one hand, holding it steady like a bronze bust.

Longhair spoke. "You will drink, one way or another. It's easier if you do it voluntarily. It's not poison. It will help you sleep. You need sleep."

She took the glass. The smell was chemical, bitter. She raised it for a sip, but the Animal tilted her hand and forced the liquid down her throat.

It seared like paint.

He took the empty glass and pulled her backward, pressing on her head again. She resisted, but her strength was gone.

Dimly, she saw the blond unzip the canvas bag.

The Animal said something in Russian.

She understood instantly.

"I'm having this one," he said.

The phone in Vronsky's jacket trilled.

"You got her?" a voice asked—Texas vowels, broad and drawled.

"We have," Vronsky said, pressing the phone close under his

hair. "You'll have the file soon."

Silence.

He continued, "No problems at this time."

"The Tuesday a.m. deadline isn't moveable."

"You'll get video tonight. As arranged."

"I'm waiting."

The call ended.

Semyon and Yuri were in the other room with the girl. Vronsky moved quickly to join them. He didn't trust Semyon around women—especially helpless ones.

She lay unconscious on the motel bed, limbs splayed.

Semyon, still watching her, said, "She has tasty *bufera*. Some of the best I've seen."

Yuri clucked his tongue. "She needs to stay untouched."

"She excites me."

Semyon's talent for terrifying hostages had value. His impulse to sample female ones was a problem. In the past, it had been manageable. Now, he wore an air of entitlement, like he deserved fringe benefits.

Vronsky wasn't confident the girl would come through unscathed. He'd try to restrain Semyon, but if things went wrong—well, not all kidnappings ended cleanly. That was the nature of the job.

"Put the chains and tape on before she wakes," he said.

Semyon looped dog chains around the bed legs, brought the ends to her wrists, spread her arms, and fastened them with nylon ties. A six-inch strip of duct tape sealed her mouth. He worked with grim efficiency.

Her dress had ridden up. Yuri tugged the hem down.

"You scared of seeing something exciting?" Semyon said.

Vronsky stepped in, throwing an arm around his shoulder. "Let's talk in the other room. She might be faking, might understand."

"What does it matter?" Semyon muttered but let himself be led away.

"Once we're done here," he added, "we scoot home. No one touches us."

Vronsky shut the door behind them.

So far, so smooth.

They'd been hired in Moscow by a man calling himself Mr. Robert—vetted by trusted contacts, confirmed as a genuine client, not FSB or police.

The job was simple: snatch the girl, film her, hold her a few days, release her.

Vronsky's background checks revealed Mr. Robert's real identity: Bobby Flint, majority shareholder of Flint Oil Services—an independent contractor tied to major oil and gas companies. Based in Houston. Drilling contracts worldwide.

"He didn't explain the situation," Vronsky had told the others. "But it's clear he's applying pressure on someone. It's not about money—he wants the girl released after. So he must have leverage to stop anyone from going to the FBI."

Which meant no deaths. Deaths made things messier. And Semyon Grigori Nikitin was a walking complication.

A boulder of a man, he'd perfected the art of terror during Soviet campaigns in Afghanistan. When a village needed pacifying, they sent in Semyon's unit. Survivors were too traumatized to describe what happened.

Rape was a favorite tool. Mutilation, a message.

"This is how we remember our enemies," Semyon once announced to a crowd of horrified villagers. He tied an old man to one tank tread, a boy to the other. Signaled the commander to drive. The shrieks of Afghan women rising over the grind of metal stayed with Vronsky forever.

Two lives crushed in seconds. That had been Semyon's proudest moment.

Vronsky knew this—he was his commander for three years.

Flint had paid $250,000 upfront. Provided photos and tracking data. The rest of the $1 million would come after proof of captivity was delivered via video.

They'd watched the girl for two days. She followed a pattern: left home at 8 a.m., returned late afternoon. One night, a man dropped her off around ten—boyfriend or regular date. They kissed at the door. She went in alone. The man drove off in an old Mustang.

Vronsky decided they'd break in and wait. If the boyfriend came in too—he didn't look like a threat.

"This contact," Yuri had said, "he must have good connections. It took him one day to get keys to her house. Why use us if he has top-level access?"

Yuri Maksim Buteyko, ex-FSB and administrator for the job, always wanted to know more than necessary.

"Businessmen and politicians take risks," Vronsky replied. "So they avoid official channels. All he needs is a crew who can kidnap quietly. That's what we offer."

Yuri had big dreams. Wanted to run his own crew someday. Vronsky knew it wouldn't happen.

Sure, Yuri had good U.S. connections. Smart, too. But not rat smart. Not the kind of cunning needed to survive in their world.

His background was soft. Well-placed parents got him a

cushy FSB post. He'd never clawed for survival. The privileged never do.

He also spent too much time in front of mirrors. Vronsky wondered what that said about him.

"You think we'll be done by Tuesday?" Yuri asked.

He liked order. Schedules. Checklists.

Vronsky had put him in charge of logistics—knew he'd be efficient, even if whiny.

"If we don't have order," Yuri liked to say, "chaos will reign." He said a lot of rubbish like that.

He hadn't been the first choice for this op. But better men weren't available.

"I said we deliver the video before Tuesday," Vronsky replied. "What happens after, we wait to hear. A decision is being made that day."

"What kind of decision?"

"Our man's involved in a gas deal here. Big money. He'll need a top-level signature. That's what the girl's about. He didn't share documents, but I get the picture."

"How long will it take? I need to book flights."

"Probably a few days after Tuesday. I negotiated for a fast job, not a drawn-out hostage drama. We send the video, then wait for the release signal. That's all I know."

Vronsky poured vodka into tumblers and passed them around.

"*Nazdrovie*," he said. "To health."

"*Nazdrovie*," the others echoed, and drained their glasses.

"A few days," Semyon said. "Enough time to know her thoroughly."

"Let's not have a messy situation," Yuri said. "Keep it clean.

Clinical."

"Forget the girl," Vronsky told Semyon. "Think of the money."

"Our money?" Semyon said, voice sour. "When I think of it, I think of one thing: you get most of it."

CHAPTER 2

Zachary Bones pushed through the 14th-floor entrance of the Chicago Post and nodded at the two women on reception. Mid-afternoon. Eight hours to deadline. The place crackled with nervous energy.

Faces were taut with tension. Staffers who once sauntered now strode, conferring in clipped tones, heads close.

Not him.

He had no story for this edition—or the next. His last big piece, an exposé on cops pocketing pimps' earnings instead of arresting them, had earned him some breathing space. A grudging nod from the City Editor. If left alone, he might just land another hit.

Corruption, incompetence, plain stupidity—Zach skewered local officials for all of it. The result? Several departments hated him. He didn't mind. In a masochistic way, he enjoyed it.

"I worry about you," Keera had said once. "You take on dangerous people."

He'd laughed. "Me? I had a peaceful life until I met you. A

few angry politicians calling the editor—that was the worst of it. Then you drag me out of my body to some terrifying place where I nearly get stabbed six ways before breakfast. I still don't know if that was a dream or not. I just know it worries me you could talk me into it again."

"That was a special case."

The day they met. She'd told him time travel was possible—if you left your body. He'd humored her. Then he found himself in a Sioux camp, two centuries in the past. Helping her recover a Sacred Stone. Falling for her. Making it back to sanity—and grateful just to know her.

"I know you think psychics and mediums are fringe wackos," she'd said. "It surprises me we're still together. Must be hard reconciling your beliefs with your actions."

Her stare had been unreadable, unsettling. Was she questioning his commitment? Joking?

She was the most perfect creature he'd ever seen. Mind sharpened by elite education, body Photoshopped by God. He'd adored her from day one. Every minute since only deepened his awe.

"I respect your abilities," he'd said. "It's just… what you do is illogical. It doesn't fit with any rational view of the world. I can't wrap my head around how you accept the dead and the living just hanging out together."

"You get it," she said, smiling. "You just won't admit it. People might talk, yes?"

"You don't exactly ring your bell about it either. 'A career to protect,' you said."

"A girl's got to eat, Zach. The dead don't hand out food parcels."

He hadn't pointed out that her father—an oil exec—had set

her up with a trust fund worth millions. She didn't need to work. Anthropology research was her pastime. She wasn't one to idle in luxury, but she could have if she wanted. Unlike him.

He'd grown up with radical-left parents in a cramped one-bedroom flat. Every penny he had, he'd earned. Then spent.

They were nothing alike, in background or temperament. He couldn't figure out why she stayed with him.

Now, he pulled out his phone and dialed her. No answer. A recorded message: The number you are calling is out of range or switched off.

Keera never turned her phone off. Never forgot to charge it. He tried her landline. It rang, and rang, and rang. She must still be in a meeting or something.

They both had the next day off—Friday. Planned to kick-start the long weekend with a late lunch. He hoped she wasn't bringing work home.

Twenty minutes later, still no response. He set the phone down, hit the power button on his computer. He couldn't concentrate until she called, but pretending to work beat doing nothing.

"Hey," he said to Howard, who sat next to him. "Anything exciting from City Hall today? Or just the usual furtive pocket-lining?"

Howard Hossack. New to the section. Crisp hair, Ralph Lauren wardrobe, a knack for writing clean, publishable copy. Destined to be a political columnist, probably. Nobody chose words more carefully.

He covered local government, like Zach. But while Zach got scoops from insiders, Howard rewrote press releases into readable prose.

"They've allocated extra money to clean up graffiti in playgrounds," Howard said, eyes on his screen, fingers flying.

"The mayor's against kids expressing themselves?" Zach asked. "Who got the contract?"

"Press release doesn't say."

"Funny, that. Let me know when they announce it. I'll check if the company's tied to whoever approved the deal."

Howard looked up. "No faith in government? Just because a million bucks pops up for a non-issue project, you think it's shady?"

"I'd need to stop thinking to believe otherwise."

Zach drained his lukewarm latte, tossed the cup in the bin, and eyed the stack of cuttings on his desk. Some had notes scribbled across them—Edwina Moss's handwriting. "Mrs. Ed" to the team. Meticulous, picky even.

They'd worked together at CityScape, a Chicago entertainment mag that died under the weight of internet competition. Both were fired the same day by a luckless new owner who had to shut the place within a year.

Zach had landed at *The Post*—and, to his dismay, so had Edwina. She became his editor again.

Oddly, she seemed to have left old grudges behind. Misfortune, it turned out, was a great equalizer.

He considered calling Keera again, resisted, then caved. Same message. Tried her landline. Endless ringing. Again, nothing.

He dropped the phone in his pocket, leaned back. Howard noticed.

"Something wrong? You look unsettled."

"Trying to reach a friend. It's taking a while."

Zach skimmed his inbox. A message from Lyndon, a college

buddy now in London as a merchant banker—the same guy who cost him ten grand with a bad horse tip. But over time, better tips followed. Losses turned into gains. The winnings sat in a UK bookie's account, tricky to transfer without raising IRS flags.

Lyndon had a solution: an offshore account in the Bahamas.

"It's yours for a thousand bucks," he'd said. "I'll send the number and password. Perfect place to park your winnings."

Zach wired the money. Now he had a secret account in paradise.

He called Keera again. Same result.

Something began to gnaw inside.

They'd agreed not to live together, and it worked—for the most part. He stayed over on weekends. He wanted more. She'd said, "I want to always be glad to see you. I don't want to get used to having you around."

She was right.

He spent weeknights at his place. She spent hers researching —astral travel, she called it. Said her guide Bardo showed her things, took her places. He didn't understand it, didn't want to. She said it would take forever to explain. He was fine with that.

"I don't get it all yet either," she'd added. "I'm being taught things that still don't make sense."

They never would to him.

He checked the time. He could sit and wait—or do something.

With no story in the next issue, production staff didn't need him. He decided to drive to her place.

"Gotta go," he said to Howard, standing and shutting his computer.

"You just got here," Howard said, still typing. "Well, I expect you'll return."

"Course I will. I work here. But right now, I need to find someone."

"Don't we all?" Howard waved a lazy goodbye.

Zach pulled up near Keera's vintage townhouse and bounded up the front steps.

He opened the door and knew instantly the place was empty. Her presence, so tangible to him even when he couldn't see her in the next room, was missing.

"Keera?" he called. "Keera?"

No answer.

Then he saw it.

Through the living room doorway, on the coffee table, her handbag, open with the content scattered over the coffee table. His alarm doubled, then trebled.

Two bottles of vodka on the mantel. Three shot glasses—two on the mantel, one on the coffee table—plus a tumbler.

Stolichnaya.

Keera didn't drink hard liquor. Maybe wine, occasionally.

No sign she had expected guests. Which meant—maybe—they weren't expected.

And no woman left home without her handbag. Not willingly. Not like this.

Zach knelt. Examined the glasses. A trace of liquid remained—clear, sharp-scented. Vodka. But the tumbler smelled bitter.

Not alcohol for pleasure. Something else.

He searched the house anyway, but found nothing to settle him. No sign of forced entry. No Keera.

Panic pressed in.

He called her department at the University of Chicago.

"Department of Anthropology," a woman said.

"Hi, can you put me through to Ms Miles?"

"She's gone for the day."

"What time did she leave?"

"I can't share that."

"I'm her partner. She's missing. This is not normal."

A pause.

"I'm sorry, sir. Perhaps you should call the police."

"Fine. If she returns, please tell her Zach Bones called."

He gave his number and hung up.

The police. What could he tell them?

My girlfriend hasn't called me? Left her purse behind?

The fridge held two Heinekens. He drank one, then the other. Tried her phone again. Still off.

Her laptop was on the kitchen table. He logged in.

Internet working. Gmail opened automatically.

Recent emails—mundane. A few from students, a couple between them. No red flags.

He closed the laptop.

He called the closest hospital.

"My friend hasn't come home. Any accidents involving a Keera Miles?"

No admissions under that name, sir. Tried three more. Nothing.

Upstairs, her robe lay on the bed. His side untouched, waiting for the weekend.

He stared at the bed, hoping for inspiration. Nothing came. Only the idea he didn't want.

He left the house.

And drove straight to the local precinct—the worst place to ask for help.

CHAPTER 3

The chink-chink of chains registered first. A white ceiling swam into view, then veered sideways. Keera blinked. The ceiling stayed where it was.

She moved her arm. Her wrists jerked against restraints. Chains. Tape over her mouth—sticky, claustrophobic.

She turned her head left, then right. Staked out like a trophy. Tried to sit up. Chains yanked her back. The room swayed. She shut her eyes until the spinning stopped.

Her throat was dry, her tongue thick. Those Russians. Those bastards. That drink.

A motel. Cheap prints on the wall. Beige everything. Generic furniture. She craned her head and spotted the embossed information folder on the bedside table. Yep—motel. No visible address. Not that it would help. They hadn't blindfolded her, so they didn't care if she knew where she was.

Did that mean they didn't expect her to live? She pushed the thought aside. They said a few days. And then?

Why am I here? she asked Bardo.

No reply.

She was never sure when he would answer. But now? Now he was silent?

Her early years were guided by others—strange presences who appeared when she was just a girl, when she first started seeing the dead and receiving visions she couldn't explain. Later, when she learned to manage those gifts, Bardo had appeared.

"You're it? My new guide?" she'd said, stunned to find a rotund monk sitting on her couch, his bowl haircut lopsided, his robe stained with food.

"This was my outward form in my past life," he'd said with a slow smile. "I kept the look. I can stay immaterial, if you prefer."

"It's okay. I can live with this."

Bardo made it clear she wasn't his first choice to guide. He'd heard talk. She was difficult, headstrong even, but he had no option and could she be a little more cooperative with him, please?

"I have my own life to lead," she told him once.

"Of course," he'd nodded. "I'm only here to help."

Most of the time. Except now.

I'm tired. Drugged. I need help. Please, Bardo. Say something.

Silence.

A meaningful silence. His way of saying: You have what you need.

She listened. No footsteps. No chains on the door. The men must be in other rooms. Her watch was missing. Weak daylight filtered through the curtains. Late afternoon, maybe.

Zach would be looking for her. Talking to the police. But it wouldn't be long enough for them to call her missing. Another twenty-four hours, maybe.

And her father? He had the money and the influence to mobilize a search. But he didn't even know she was missing. Zach didn't have a contact number for him. She hadn't told her father about Zach.

Still, Zach was relentless. Tenacious. He'd dig until he got results. Until then, she had only herself. Her one advantage: the ability to leave her body.

Few mediums could do it at will. For her, it started at puberty. Bardo helped. Took her to places beyond imagining. By her twenties, she could travel anywhere she could think of. No luggage. No body.

Now she had to go.

She relaxed. The drug fuzz still clung to her, but maybe not enough to stop her. She waited for the in-between moment—that thin slip between waking and sleeping, when the sense of body vanishes. That's when the consciousness lifts.

She waited. Tried not to doze.

Nothing.

Then, a whoosh. She was out. Floating. Ceiling inches from her face.

She drifted through the wall. Felt the layers: paint, plaster, wood. Entered the main room.

Three men chewed pizza. Two empty boxes on the table. One slice left in a third.

"She'll be awake soon," the Animal said.

"I'll have a look."

"Leave her, Semyon," said the long-haired one, still chewing. "Don't scare her. I don't want her jumpy."

"I'll go," the thin man said, rising.

"Fine. But, Yuri, don't touch her. These types hate it."

"I'm not a groper like him," Yuri said.

Semyon laughed. "Sure you're not still a virgin, Buteyko?"

Earlier, they'd spoken English. Enough Russian between them that she could grasp. But now—in this form—she understood everything. Even what they didn't say. Their emotions coiled around them, visible like auras. They were working together, but not close.

She floated behind Yuri as he stepped into her room. He bent over her.

Please don't touch me.

If he touched her, she'd snap back into her body. Maybe for good if they pumped her with more drugs.

He picked up the motel brochure from the bedside table and left.

She followed.

"Who left this beside her?" he asked, waving the folder.

Vronsky took it. "Was she still asleep?"

Yuri nodded. "Lucky for us."

He glanced at Semyon, who shrugged. "I was carrying the bitch. I can't do all the housework."

"Never mind," Vronsky said, clearly eager to avoid conflict. "No harm done."

He took the last slice of pizza.

"If she's not awake in half an hour, we start anyway. Once the video's sent, we wait for the word to release her."

"When does he pay?" Semyon asked.

"Not until the money's in my account. That much, Mister Texas Oil agreed."

"What if he doesn't pay?"

"Then we kill the girl. Then find and kill him."

But Vronsky was distracted. A flicker of something else. She caught the image: a young man. His son, maybe. He was worried. Deeply. And he kept that worry hidden from the others.

She felt the tug. The pull back to her body. It never could be ignored.

She jerked awake. Her throat burned.

But now she had something. Names. And a reason.

Her father.

A solitary butterball in uniform eyed Zach as he stepped up to the precinct counter. A tired couple sat nearby, hollowed out by waiting, drained of expectations.

"Zachary Bones. *Chicago Post.* I want to report a missing person."

The cop stared for thirty seconds, then: "Zachary Bones?"

He nodded.

"From the *Chicago Post?*"

"What is this, a hearing test?"

The cop leaned back and shouted, "Hey Sarge! There's a guy here you should meet. Zachary Bones."

A pinched face poked around the corner, followed by a uniform draped over a bony frame. The man glided up until his face was inches from Zach's.

"You the guy who wrote that shit about the 19th?"

"The ones shaking down hookers and pimps? Disgrace to the badge? Yeah. That was me."

Six months old, that story. But cops had long memories.

"You ruined some good men. Your name still comes up."

"Anyone pass a hat for me? Buy me something nice?"

"What crap are you pulling now?"

"Missing person."

"Not you, apparently. What a pity." Sarge waved to the desk cop who strolled over with a notebook

"Name of the missing person?" he asked.

"Keera Miles."

Desk Cop scribbled. "Miles like highways? K-E-I-R-A?"

"Two Es. No I."

Scribble. Scratch.

"Relation?" Sarge asked.

"She's a friend."

Sarge lit up. "So your girlfriend dumped you, and you want us to find her?"

"She was due to meet me. Didn't call. Didn't show. Her phone's off. Her handbag's still at home. Contents scattered. I have strong reasons to believe something's happened to her."

"Maybe she just ran. From you."

Zach said, "I'm reporting a possible kidnapping and you're making a joke of it?"

The Sarge grunted at the desk guy. "Norman still around?"

"Yeah."

"Give him this worm."

Desk Guy picked up the phone. "Norman? Sarge wants you."

Moments later, Norman strolled out. Street clothes. Squared frame. The department's middle ground between emaciated and inflated.

"Detective Norman Horn, sir. How can I help you?"

Zach needed cooperation from this guy, and he was being offered a fresh start. He surpassed the inner rancor Sarge had activated and repeated his story.

Horn nodded. "Most of these cases sort themselves out.

Adults disappear all the time. Did you two have a fight?"

"No."

"Let's see if she shows up tonight. Call around. Maybe she's with friends. If not, we'll knock on some doors tomorrow."

Plodding procedure. Keera could be dead and buried before they completed the first piece of paperwork.

Then Horn added, "Those cops you busted? They weren't evil. Just tempted. Could happen to anyone. Even you."

"Sure."

Horn let it drop. Pulled out a tin can.

"Want to donate to the Police Orphans Fund?"

A dollar-store can covered in dollar signs.

Zach peeled a bill from his pocket and dropped it in.

"Thanks. Appreciate your help."

"Wow. A whole dollar," Desk Guy said as Zach walked out.

If Horn replied, the door closed before Zach heard it.

CHAPTER 4

Keera lay chained and spread-eagled on a motel bed, three strange men in the next room. Panic pushed at the edges, but she fought it down. She had to stay in control, analyze the situation, and plan a way out. Steady breaths. Visualize protective light.

Her father. That's why she was here. Nelson Miles—Chief Operating Officer at Prime Resources Corporation, one of the world's top twenty oil and gas firms. He awarded the contracts for construction and maintenance of rigs. Contracts worth hundreds of millions.

She hated the industry—never asked about his work during their rare meetings—but she knew enough. These men weren't after her. They were after him. Or someone connected to him.

"If bribery were legal," he'd once joked, "I could have retired years ago."

She didn't believe he'd ever taken a bribe. He was upright, if emotionally absent. A decent man in a morally grey industry. As a father, he had the parenting skills of a doorstop. She'd learned not to expect affection.

Her English mother accepted the trade-off—status and money for a ghost of a husband. Lunches and shopping filled her days.

Keera's childhood was lonely. Her stories about seeing the dead excited her friends—until her family moved again. Friendships dissolved. After a while, she stopped trying. Self-analysis told her she'd never learned intimacy.

Then Bardo brought Zach.

We like him. You need him, Bardo had said.

She'd resisted, but Zach slipped past her defenses—a wisecracking realist drawn to the darker corners of life. He broke through, and stayed. She liked him more than she expected. Maybe loved him, though she wasn't sure what that felt like.

"You're such a loner," he said once. "Six months, and I still don't know you."

In a rare confession, she'd blurted: "I don't expect people to stay. I keep myself prepared."

He'd flinched, but covered it with a joke. She felt his pain—and that surprised her more than the words. His emotions had become hers. He was wary of the psychic stuff, but he respected it. Probably wished it weren't real.

"I never had a choice," she told him. "I was born like this. I'll die like this."

Now, her abilities were her only card.

The Russians said they'd video her. Not for her father—he'd never respond directly. But someone else would. Someone who could pressure him. Probably a business rival. The deal must be huge. She figured they'd already tried bribery. It failed.

Now they were trying something more persuasive. No father

could ignore a kidnapped daughter. Not without public shame. Even if he didn't want her, the media would crucify him for inaction.

They said she'd be held a few days. So they expected an answer soon. That gave her a timeline. The Russians were professionals, yes. But they had the stink of death about them. She felt it. They had killed before.

The door opened. Vronsky stood there.

"You're awake. Good. We have movie to make."

Not porn. Please, not porn.

He crossed the room. "I remove tape. You stay quiet. If you scream, we film with tape on. And you suffer. Understand?"

She nodded. Hostage video, then.

He ripped off the tape. Her mouth burned. He unchained one wrist and pulled her upright. She curled into herself, arms crossed, muscles aching.

"The princess ready yet?" Semyon leaned in from the hallway, holding a newspaper. His gaze raked over her and stayed.

"Hold front page out," Vronsky told her "You say, 'I am safe and well. Please follow instructions.'"

"You want ransom? From who? How much?" Keera asked, her lips burning from the tape removal.

"Confidential. Best you not know. Sit quiet. We set scene."

Yuri entered with water. She drank. Asked for more. He brought it. A soft touch, for a kidnapper. She sipped slowly. Each swallow tightened her psychic link. Her powers returned in layers. The room was warm, but she didn't want to remove her jacket, it felt like some protection. Semyon hadn't taken his eyes off her.

"How much, and from whom?" she asked again.

Vronsky ignored her, pulled her phone from his pocket, switched it on, thumbed a few buttons until he found what he wanted. He peered at the screen while pointing the phone at her. "It's good. Quite a wide angle and low down, but it's clear who's talking. We can't all be Oscar winners. The newspaper please."

Semyon unfolded the *Chicago Post*.

"Hold it to lens," Vronsky said.

Semyon shoved the paper into her chest. His knuckles grazed her breast.

She grabbed it and sailed it across the room. Before it hit the ground, a sharp crack across her face knocked her sideways off the bed, the chain snatching at her wrist. Her cheek flamed, and she blinked to refocus. She dabbed her face with the back of her hand to cool it. What did they hit her with, a leather strap?

Almost the same thing--Semyon's heavy, meaty hand.

Vronsky retrieved the paper. Refolded it. Held it out.

"Front page facing phone."

She climbed back onto the bed shaking, and took the paper.

"Say words. Before bruise show."

"I have forgotten them."

"I am safe and well. Please follow instructions."

She drank the last of the water. Tried to focus. Once, she'd been photographed in a trance. The image blurred. Maybe it would happen again. Any disruption helped. Slow breaths. Visualize the light. Open each chakra. Slide into trance. Less than sixty seconds. Usually.

"Ready?" Vronsky said. "Tilt newspaper down on left."

He tapped the phone. Watched.

Keera, oblivious to him, eyes closed, working deep in her zone, the buzz enveloping her, telling her she was moving out of the normal world.

"*Nyet!*"

His bark shattered her focus. She jerked, eyes blinking. Semyon stood closer now.

"Just say words."

His face hardened with impatience.

"I am safe and well. Please follow instructions."

He replayed the video. Cursed. "Out of focus. Looks like anyone." He fiddled with settings. "I try night mode. Say it again."

She was out of the trance now. Couldn't get back. She spoke the line in monotone.

Vronsky replayed. Grinned. "Clear. Thank you, Miss Miles."

He switched off the phone and left. Yuri stayed. Semyon rechained her, reapplied the tape. Took his time. Let his hands brush her breasts again and again. She forced herself not to flinch.

When they shut the door behind them, she closed her eyes, deflated and defeated. Only Zach would know something was wrong. She wasn't due back at the university until Monday. No one else would miss her.

Hospitals. Police. Maybe Zach had found clues. Maybe he sensed something off. He knew her rhythms. Knew she didn't have guests. He might guess.

"I guide you," Bardo said suddenly. "Others guide him."

She lifted her head. He was there. Curled in a chair, robes stained, bowl cut as uneven as ever. Smiling like a favorite uncle.

"I thought you'd abandoned me," she said silently.

"Oh no. Still time to run."

He brushed imaginary crumbs from his robe. The stains remained.

"You mean years? I'll get away?"

"Time means more to you than to me. Past, present, future—it's the same day in different directions."

"Will I survive?"

"You'll live forever. Haven't I taught you that much?"

She kicked the bedframe. "You know what I mean. Don't get metaphysical."

He waited. Made her ask precisely.

"Will they kill me? Will they—?" her voice trailed off as dark and ugly images swamped her.

"The future is fluid."

Gee thanks. "What are their plans?"

"Depends on Zach."

"How do I get him to help me?"

"He's already searching."

She saw him—a brief flash—arguing with cops, pacing, fuming. She felt his agitation. It echoed in her. "He needs help. He's untrained."

"His motivation is high," Bardo said. "He's ready to go the next step."

"Like what?"

Bardo didn't answer. His glowing outline shimmered blue-white. Then he faded, leaving an empty chair.

CHAPTER 5

Zach pulled his car into the *Post's* parking garage, killed the engine, and slammed the steering wheel with the heel of his hand. He tried Keera's home number again —no signal. Of course. Too far underground.

He caught the elevator to the fourteenth floor. Howard was filing papers into a knee-high cabinet, his desk already cleared.

Zach nodded a greeting, peeled off his jacket, and draped it over his chair. His phone lit up with reception. He tried her home again. It rang endlessly. Her mobile went straight to voicemail.

Is she okay? Alive, even?

Howard might know. The guy knew everything.

"Howard, help me out. How do you find out if someone's alive or dead?"

"Try the Social Security Death Index."

"I meant something more immediate. Like a 'who died today' hotline."

"Hospitals?"

"Tried them. Nothing."

"Police?"

"Yeah. Not what you'd call empathetic."

Howard raised an eyebrow. "Recognized your name, did they?"

"Something like that." Zach straightened. "This is serious. Keera's missing. Nobody's heard from her. I'm getting edgy as hell."

"Since when?"

"This afternoon. She was supposed to call. Never did. I went to her place—handbag still there. Vodka bottles on the table. Enough glasses for four people. And..."

"You think something bad happened? Based on that?"

"You see another conclusion?"

Howard leaned back, skeptical. "You think she was snatched?"

"Jesus, don't say it like that. Makes my skin crawl." Images of porn movies, filled with sadism and pain, snuff movies for God's sake, unreeled in his head.

"Maybe she got caught up in something. She'll call."

"It's out of character. Leaving her handbag? That's not Keera."

"Okay, valid point," Howard said. He tapped a pencil against his desk. "You don't trust the cops to act fast?"

"Not fast enough. They won't move for twenty-four hours. I can't wait that long."

Howard gave him a look. "Didn't you say Keera's psychic? She ever teach you anything useful? Might help now."

Zach exhaled hard. "You think I'm into that stuff?"

"You're dating someone who is."

"I'm drawn to her, not the woo-woo."

"So if you infiltrated a Klan rally, you'd be drawn to white supremacist?"

Zach winced. "Okay, okay. I get it. Stay focused. How would I contact her—psychically?"

"You don't have to be advanced. Just open."

"You're one of them, aren't you?"

"Not exactly. Just curious about how the mind works."

"You read books on astral travel, man. You browse ghost sites."

"Because I want answers. Explain poltergeists, ghosts, objects flying through air in a closed room. Until someone does, I go with the best theory: consciousness after death. Simpler than the alternatives."

Zach rubbed his eyes. "I don't have enough coffee for this."

"Do you want help or not?"

"Yes. Ideas?"

"Try a spiritualist church."

Zach blinked. "Those still exist? Table rapping and ectoplasm shows?"

"Less of that now. They're mostly low-key. Hymns, messages from the dead."

Unbelievable. Keera had never asked him to believe—just to watch, observe, decide for himself. Now Howard was basically handing him a belief system.

"Even though I'm dating a psychic, I stay away from that scene. They see patterns where there aren't any. Desperate for meaning."

"Your girlfriend like that?"

"No. Keera's grounded. She questions everything—even herself. Wouldn't be caught dead in a kooky circle."

Howard didn't flinch. "Still a good place to start."

"You really think I'll find her through that? I'm not expecting her to be dead, Howard. I just want to find her."

"Then you need every option. Call a local church. They'll help you. They don't charge."

Howard turned back to his monitor. "Do it now. She might call before the service even starts."

Zach searched. First hit: The Spirituality Church of Chicago.

A cheerful woman answered. "We have a Sunday service at two. People there can help you. Look forward to seeing you!" Sunday? It was Thursday.

"We also have a service tonight at eight," she added, like she'd read his mind. "A talk and a demonstration."

He thanked her and hung up.

"She mentioned a demonstration," Zach said. "That freaky stuff you mentioned?"

"Someone gets on stage and gives messages. Usually a woman. If your friend's on the other side, and it was sudden, she'll try to make contact."

Howard stood. "I have to go. Let me know what happens."

Zach watched him leave. Howard—the preppy, bookish guy —was a low-key expert on the paranormal. Practically a feature story in himself.

His phone said he had time. He shrugged on his jacket.

He wanted to ask Howard something else but couldn't pin it down, even as he caught the elevator and drove into dusk.

He tried Keera's phone again.

"This number is not in operation at this moment," a voice intoned.

He called her landline. It rang and rang.

He imagined it echoing through her empty house.

And felt emptier still.

CHAPTER 6

Zach walked into the church hall. Inside, two women, around seventy years old, moved plastic chairs into position with all the agility of wounded cattle.

"Can I help?" he asked. The closest woman turned to him, a sweet smile breaking open.

"Of course," she replied. "We need to set out eight rows of eight for the visitors tonight."

He pulled chairs off a stack in the hallway and joined the women setting up. One dropped a stapled booklet onto each seat.

"Your first time here?" she asked.

"Yes, I'm interested in what you do."

"You'll find the evening very informative."

"A friend told me I might get a message from a loved one." He sounded desperate, but he didn't care.

She paused with a chair in her hand. "You should talk to Reverend Rachel." She pointed her chin at a woman at the front of the hall.

The Reverend Rachel was short, dressed in floral, and moved

with an industrious bustle while she stacked literature on a side table, placed a vase on the front table, and set out drinking glasses next to it. She exuded the buoyant energy of a person who loved their work.

Zach approached, seven years old again, and teacher shy. He cleared his throat. "A friend suggested I come here to receive a message."

Reverend Rachel regarded him with a crinkle of amusement in her eyes. "I see."

Perhaps it was the calm expression, or the openness, but he felt he could talk to her and not be laughed at. "I need to speak to somebody on the other side. I mean, I hope she's not there, but she might be, and I have to know." His words rushed out.

"I see," Reverend Rachel said again. "Stay the evening. I'll find someone to help afterward."

He took a seat in a row he had constructed and waited. More people arrived, shy, with nervous eye movements. Followed by a bunch of regulars, greeting the church members like they were family. The final groups were like him: those who had come reluctantly but with hope. He saw it in the way they held themselves, not open, but trying not to close off the door to their souls.

He couldn't imagine Keera in this place. She was careful to hide her abilities from others, and it was only because her guide Bardo insisted she join up with Zach for a particular mission a year ago that they came together at all.

He'd had to make an enormous leap of faith just to believe the paranormal was, in fact, quite normal. His training and logical mindset stopped him from taking too much on trust. He needed solid proof of all assertions, and Keera couldn't provide them.

"Nobody can," she explained once. "This isn't something for science. It's beyond that. That's why it's hard to establish principles. Maybe in a hundred years we'll understand more. Right now, I use what I have and it never lets me down."

The mediums assembled themselves, after exchanging hugs and kisses on arrival, at a long table up front. Reverend Rachel rose and said, "We'll start with a song to lift the energy in the room. You'll find the words in the booklet we put out for you on the seats. I'm sure you know most of the songs already."

She pushed a button on a small round CD player. Zach recognized the opening bars of the Carpenters' "Close to You." He would never forget it. His father sang it in the shower every morning. Sang it the worst it could be sung.

Not the same result here. Voices added to voices, and the melody gathered strength as the people sang as if the song spoke personally to them.

Afterward, they all sat and Reverend Rachel started. "We're lucky to have a new medium with us tonight—Shirley. But first, the news. Next Saturday we have a workshop in grounding and chakras, seeing energy and auras. The fee is a reasonable sixty dollars. Please call Fleur if you wish to attend. Her number is on our website. Following that, we'll have another workshop in channeling energy, and healing the mind, body and spirit. You have to attend the first workshop before you can attend the second, and Fleur will decide if you're ready."

That sounded reasonable to him. Letting people channel before they were grounded could complicate lives.

"Bring a cushion and a blanket," Rachel added. "It's cold in here when the portals are open. Now, here's Shirley. She's very good at overheads."

"What are overheads?" Zach whispered to the skinny girl sitting next to him, pleasant-faced, in her twenties, the backpacker type.

"That means the medium sees points of light over certain people, and she knows these are the ones she's to address her message to," she whispered back. Sounded pretty knowledgeable, and he made a note to chat with her later.

Shirley stood and smiled at her audience. Stoutly breasted and confident, with frizzed-out black hair, she carried the air of a colonel inspecting her troops. She waited; the audience waited with her. "I've got an Agnes here. Agnes, anyone? Or a Paul?"

A Paul. Sounded like Agnes wasn't pushy enough to get her message through.

Somebody raised a hesitant hand.

Shirley said, "I'm getting that he's passed over recently, and he was related to your mother's side."

The head belonging to the hand nodded.

"He sends love, and says not to worry, he's fine. He's with your Uncle Ben. Does that make sense?"

The head nodded more vigorously.

"You'll get what you need when you travel, he says. Also, speak up in the future. People will listen to you. Don't be surprised. Bless you," Shirley said, swung her gaze around the room and settled on Zach.

He froze. No, no message, please. Not from anyone, especially not from Keera. No message from Keera was the best news possible. Shirley looked at him speculatively for a few more seconds before asking the whole room, "I have a Dot here. I can't understand her very well, but she's insisting there's a girl here she's related to."

The backpacker sitting next to Zach raised her hand. "I have a grandmother in spirit. Her name was Dottie."

"She prefers Dot," Shirley said crisply, "and she has a message."

Shirley paused again. Zach guessed Dot was formulating a long message.

"She says you and your partner lived together in a previous life. She's showing me a picture of the two of you in a medieval market. Selling apples. You're both very poor but happy."

The backpacker beamed with such intensity Zach sensed the heat. "Thank you so much," she said, delighted.

A half hour and a dozen messages later, Shirley thanked and blessed the audience and concluded the evening. People stood, some left, others headed for the coffee machine and cookies on a back table. A bowl carried a note suggesting a donation of ten dollars. A handful of small bills already lay there.

The backpacker dropped a five in the bowl. A bargain to know your partner was one you already had the same arguments with in a previous life. Zach pulled out a five and added to the pile. "Interesting news about your partner," he said to her.

"Oh, it was heaps good news," she said. "I had that feeling from the start that Gus and I were meant to be together, and tonight's just confirmed it."

"Gus isn't here tonight. Isn't he into this kind of thing?"

"He's back in California, he's got to work. I'm heading for New York, going to hang out for a while. Got friends there. He's going to join me next week."

"You going to tell him you two were an item some time ago?"

"Uh uh. Gus would freak out." She cocked her head to one side. "Nobody came through for you. You disappointed?"

Disappointed, no. Relieved, yes. "The person I want to find isn't dead, just missing. I'm hoping somebody here will help me find her."

"Oh, they can do that," she assured him. "You could even do that yourself."

"How?"

"Once, Gus got all snippy about something and left me for a couple of days. I didn't know where to find him. So I just lay down and tried to visualize him. I got a picture in my head of him at the Y. When he came home, I didn't ask, but he told me that's where he'd gone."

"The YMCA?"

She nodded. "You could do that, too. I feel it."

Helpful mediums were everywhere. "Feel it? Like in a psychic sense?"

"Exactly. I'm not as good as Shirley and the others, but I get stuff now and again. You should try it if you have the gift."

"Haven't, I'm afraid," he said. "I'll just have to struggle on like the rest of the world."

She eyed him quizzically, not sure if he was making fun of her.

Somebody touched his arm. Shirley. "Come with me," she said and led him to a back room. Two chairs sat side by side. Boxes of paperwork and files lined the walls. A heavy curtain covered the window. Shirley switched on a lamp in the corner, and turned off the overhead light, leaving a soft red glow.

"Take a seat." She waved at a chair. "I've had someone around me all night," she said. "It had different energy, very strong, not like I'm used to. He, it was a male energy, asked that I give you a private moment. What he had to say wasn't for anyone else."

"He's here now?" Zach resisted the urge to look around for an invisible man.

"Oh yes. Let's find out what he wants. Just bear with me." She stared off at nothing for a full minute before she spoke again. "I'm told this is about your girlfriend. I get a K, a Keela, a Karina or similar."

Jesus, this was unexpected. Getting her name like that. "Close enough. Where is she?"

"She's on this plane, hasn't passed."

Terrific news. Also stupid. The woman's words had meaning only if he surrendered his common sense. Information from a dead person was not normally a reliable news source. But she had brought up Keera's name without prompting. That counted for something. What else could she offer?

Shirley cocked her head. "She can't reach you, but she wants to."

"How do I find her? Where is she?"

"I have a picture of an apartment. Outside, opposite it, there's a warehouse with a roll-up shutter. It advertises appliance repairs."

"I need more than that," he said. A solid lead he could chase. Something better than waiting, his heart shrinking by the hour.

Shirley paused again. "I'm getting two fives very strongly."

"Does that mean 55th Street or an apartment number?"

"The street. Definitely the street."

"That's a long street." How many apartment blocks lined it and which of them held Keera?

"There are men with her." Shirley watched his reaction as she added, "They hold her there."

Jesus. Images of Keera in the hands of porn merchants

swarmed back. "Can you give me anything else on her whereabouts?" he asked.

Shirley waited. He waited. She brought her hands together on her lap in a gesture of finality.

"That's all I have."

"No," he said sharply. "You can't just give me disconnected bits of information. Why can't I have it all? What is happening to her? Her exact whereabouts. What you've done is make me more freaked than I was before."

"I'm sorry, but that's the way things are. I can only pass on what I get and you got all I got."

"It's not enough. You're supposed to help me, but all I got were pieces of a jigsaw. You must have more." He thought of something. "Would money help? I'm happy to pay for more information."

She gave him a patient smile. "It doesn't work like that. I can only receive what I can receive, money is irrelevant. You think I'm waffling, but even if the spirit side wants to tell me more, I may not tune in well enough to grasp it. I have limited gifts, as we all do. In any case, that spirit is no longer here."

"Is there anyone else here who could well?"

"Not at this place," Shirley said, unperturbed.

"Where can I go then?"

"Try Craigslist." She drew her feet under her as if to rise.

One other question nagged at him, and now he asked it. "Who were you communicating with? A dead relative of mine?"

"Not a relative of yours," Shirley said, standing. "Attached to your friend. His name is Bardo."

CHAPTER 7

O
ne thing Zach knew as he drove back to Keera's house: Shirley's reveals might have been frustrating and incomplete, but she'd supplied the first lead. And Bardo. She couldn't have dreamt that name up. It made the rest of her information worth investigating.

Bardo, Keera's spirit guide. Who, as she complained, mostly kept his counsel to himself.

"Not performing, eh?" Zach had said, laughing. "Ask to speak to his superior."

"Very funny. I know why he seems unhelpful sometimes: he has a different agenda to mine. It's like a parent-child relationship. A three-year-old can't understand why it can't have chocolate all the time, but the parent can. It brings a bad outcome: poor health. Likewise, when Bardo suppresses information, it's for a reason that I wouldn't grasp. He takes a longer view than I can, and if I have to pass through uncomfortable times, then it's tough but necessary."

"How uncomfortable? Uncomfortable like dying in a preventable accident that he could have warned you about?"

She didn't seem concerned about the idea. "If it's my time, then it's my time. What can I do?"

It wasn't Keera's time tonight or Bardo wouldn't have come. That was some relief. Would have been more helpful to supply a damn address. Weren't details important in the afterlife?

He thought of what he could tell the cops. Hey, Sarge, I saw a medium. She told me my girlfriend is somewhere in 55th Street. Bad guys are holding her there. Can you get on it? Guess not. Whatever he had, he was alone with it.

Once in Keera's kitchen, he switched on her laptop and opened Google Maps. Searched for appliance repairs on 55th Street. Found two. Selected Street View. Only one had a roll-up shutter. Noted the address, swung the street view through 180 degrees. An apartment block. Like Shirley had said. Holy God. The place was about fifty years old, four levels and a down ramp to the car park. Maybe 50 or 60 suites.

"Shirley," he said aloud. "I seriously apologize for my ingratitude." He scribbled the address down, grabbed his car keys and made for the front door. Stopped, returned and pulled his hoodie, t-shirt and sneakers from Keera's closet. Swapped them for his work wear of jacket, jeans and leather shoes. Best get dressed for action, leave room for movement. There might be an altercation coming up.

He paused at the living room, surveyed the mess on the coffee table in there. The Stoli bottle, the handbag contents made it look like the crime scene it was. But not a murder scene, thank God.

Zach took it slow along 55th as he approached the building numbers he had noted. Passed a strip mall, all stores closed except for a laundry, a Spanish grocery and Carlo's Liquor Store. He found the appliance place further up. Battered lettering on the shutter door declared proudly: *All Brands Repairs*. It was the same dump, no question.

Across the road was the apartment building. Four floors high. "Quest Serviced Apartments" announced a placard fixed to a scrubby patch of grass in front. Somewhere in there was Keera. If Shirley was right about the appliance joint, she was right about Keera's location. That's the crazy logic desperate men cling to. And he was no different.

A drive sloped down to an underground parking garage guarded by a steel grille. Alongside, steps led up to the main entry. Past that was a lobby behind glass doors. No concierge that he could see by the interior lights; the intercom unit on the wall connected directly to the tenants.

The building looked as it did on the laptop, didn't bear any signs of renovation in recent times. He'd written plenty of stories about construction code violations; he guessed no sophisticated elevator or security existed in a place this old. Once in, he could move to any floor.

Which floor, which suite? If he started door knocking this time of night, it would alert the kidnappers. He didn't know what they looked like. He was close to Keera, but no closer to rescuing her. Her inside somewhere, an unknown number of men with her. Drinking. Jesus, they drank while they kidnapped her. Had to be drinking now.

He swung the car around and cruised back the way he came for a few hundred yards. Stopped alongside Carlo's Liquor. A bunch of teenagers held court near the door.

"Dude," said one, a skinny Latino kid about twelve. "You pick up a Bud pack for me you can keep the change." He held a ten-dollar bill in his hand.

"Love to help," Zach said, "but me, I'm the law-abiding type. Wait until you're older for a Bud. You ain't missing much."

"Seems I'm missing a friend right now," the kid said but moved away.

Inside, the clerk had the *Post* on the counter and a sour look on his face. "You want me to list the specials? Or you just looking?"

Zach, too impatient to make nice, asked straight out, "Who bought three bottles of Stolichnaya vodka from you today or yesterday?"

"Who's asking?"

He showed his press card. "I'm doing a story on some guys from around here. The kind you don't want in your neighborhood."

"You expect me to break customer confidentiality?" For nothing, he meant.

Zach pulled out a twenty. "It'd be a public service," he said. Slid the bill across the counter. The clerk took it, stowed in his back pocket.

"What do you want to know?"

"Who bought vodkas?"

"Can't recall." Wanted more money. Was going to get some fucking grief instead.

"You see those kids out there?" Zach flicked eyes at the door. "Those kids who aren't old enough to drink?"

"Always out there. So what?"

"They told me it takes half an hour to get somebody to buy them liquor."

"That my problem?" The clerk was laughing at him now.

"They say you know about it. That sounds like a problem to me. You conspiring to break the law?"

"You're full of shit." Not laughing now.

"They said you don't always ask for ID."

The clerk waited, blinking. Journalistic highs are infrequent, but guessing something and seeing it confirmed always makes a day.

"What would happen if someone filmed these premises over a week? Would he see people coming out of your store and handing bottles to the kids? Even after I warned you this was happening?" He leaned into the counter. "What if one of those kids out there, the youngest one, just because he wanted to be a star for a day, what if he did a piece to camera saying how easy it is to get a drink around here? Do you think the licensing authorities would take action after this awful news appeared in my paper and website, and this video was out on YouTube and—"

"Every morning this week," the clerk said, "two guys come in here, not always the same two, but I've never seen more than three different ones. They buy vodka. Good stuff, Stolichnaya."

"How many times have they been here?"

"About five or six."

"What do they look like?"

The clerk held up three fingers. "Um, let's see, there's the long-haired one, there's the tall bald one and there's the one in the middle whose hair's just right."

"Young guys?"

"Older than you, say forties. The bald one looks like he can handle himself, though. No flab."

"They pay cash?" Any credit card use would identify the kidnappers if necessary.

"Pay cash, ask politely, say thank you and leave. Buy three bottles most mornings. You look like a Jack Daniels kind of guy to me."

Zach ignored the feeler, didn't need a free bottle now. "You got them on security camera?"

"It broke last week. I never seen a working one that stopped a robbery, anyway."

"Where do they come from?"

The clerk got confused. "I didn't ask for their immigration papers."

"What direction, is what I meant. But I'd like to know what nationality they are, too."

The clerk pointed east. "They come in from that way." He pointed west. "They head off that way. Getting some breakfast, I guess."

"You have any idea where they are staying?' he asked. "Think hard now."

"Let's see, they've been coming in for a week. Walk in, no car. Means they live close. Try the serviced apartments up the road. We get a lot of custom from there."

"You're very observant. What about their background?"

"I'm not the fucking FBI, man." The clerk sensing he was going to get squeezed way past his comfort level.

"Not the FBI?" Zach cocked his head. "Funny how I figured that as soon as we met. Give me your best guess about their ethnicity."

"You asking me if they were Latinos?"

Zach gave him the dead eye, and the clerk hurried to his answer.

"They had leather jackets, all of them. Figured them for Polacks at first, I get a lot of Polacks visiting relatives around here, you know. But they bought Russian vodkas. Polacks drink nothing but Polish vodkas. I'm thinking Russians."

Zach slid his business card across the counter. "Call me if they come back, right away. You got that? Right away. I wanna be here by the time they leave."

"Shit, I gotta serve 'em. Won't be time to call."

"You do the best you can." He walked to the door, stopped. "Thanks for the leads. If they run dry, I'll be back."

"Can't wait," the clerk said. "I'll bake a cake."

Outside, the kids only glanced at him as he passed them. Gone midnight and the grocery was closed, the laundry empty. The diner sign on the door stated, Open six a.m. Serving breakfast all day. Two of the Russians would come here in a few hours. He'd be ready.

Zach drove back and parked opposite the apartments with a plan. But it wasn't much of one. Follow the Russians back, right up to their floor, and see what room they entered. Call the cops and tell them he had heard a woman screaming in that room. They would respond to that. If Keera was there, and he felt sure of this, then it was game over. If not, he'd shrug and say, my mistake.

The Mustang's trunk contained a plastic toolbox. He opened it,x selected a heavy-duty box cutter. He eyed the foot-long adjustable wrench. It made him look like some repair guy if the Russians wondered who he was. It looked like a professional tool, but gripped in his hand he became a warrior.

His hand-to-hand fighting experience covered one moment. A bare-knuckle fight in a college football game where he and his tackler had thrown their helmets to the ground and swung angry, looping punches that missed their targets. He learned then that he was no boxer. Now that he was armed, he only needed anger and muscle. He had plenty of both.

His only other weapon was speed. He was a few years past his sporting peak, but he could still feint, jink, and run flat-out like a terrified deer. Found no one could catch him until he tried out for the big time. Then they all could.

But not a bunch of middle-aged Russians. He settled back in the car and waited for them to get hungry.

CHAPTER 8

Zach woke, blinked, and saw daylight. Shit. He jerked upright in his seat, joints stiff. Hadn't meant to sleep. His body had taken over, grabbing rest where it could.

Cars swished past. People spilled from the apartment block. Seven a.m. He scanned the stream of vehicles nosing up the driveway, straining to see inside. No Keera. No three men. Too many dark interiors, too many unknowns.

Had she already been moved?

He twisted to check the road—there. Two men in leather jackets turned into the strip mall. He slid out of the car and followed at a distance, keeping to the opposite side of the road.

As they reached the liquor store, he clocked them. The tubby, long-haired one bounced along; the bald one strode beside him, face as blunt and hard as a hammer.

Zach touched the box cutter in his pocket.

They entered the diner. He retreated to his car. No call from the liquor store clerk. So much for promises.

Five minutes later, the men strolled back. Baldy carried a

liquor store bag; Longhair chewed on a donut and clutched a takeout.

Zach crossed the road and fell in behind them, ten yards back, wrench in hand. Baldy glanced over his shoulder, then faced forward again.

They entered the lobby. Zach followed. The concierge desk was empty. The elevator sat idle on the third floor.

No one spoke. All three stared at the indicator lights. The elevator dinged, and a young woman stepped out, startled. She scurried past.

Longhair stepped in and pressed a button. Baldy followed, then turned.

As Zach entered, Baldy dropped the bag and lunged.

Zach twisted, ducked, scrambled backward. Baldy's grip couldn't hold him. Zach crashed out of the elevator, collided with the doors.

Swung the wrench.

It cracked across Baldy's nose—blood erupted. "Nyaargh," the Russian bellowed, stumbling.

Longhair reached inside his jacket. Gun. Had to be.

Zach drove a fist into his gut. The man doubled over.

Baldy advanced, fury in every step. Zach hurled the wrench and the cutter. The Russian blocked the wrench but the cutter smashed into his knuckles. He roared again.

Zach bolted for the stairs. He'd seen their floor button—only one had been pressed. The fourth.

He jerked open the firedoor and took the stairs two steps at a time. Maybe, just maybe, he'd beat the elevator. Even a glimpse of a closing door might give him the room number.

Below, the fire door clanged. Baldy was on him. And not slow-ing down.

Zach's lungs burned. Each breath scraped raw. He reached the fourth floor. Yanked the fire door.

Locked. Only opened from the hallway.

He tugged uselessly, then turned to face the oncoming storm.

He had the high ground. Nothing else.

Baldy slowed a few steps below, catching his breath.

The fire door squeaked open.

Longhair stood in the doorway, an automatic pointed at Zach's chest. His breaths were heavy too, but the gun was steady.

A third man—blond—stood behind him.

"You come with us," Longhair said. "Make commotion, you and your girl won't survive two seconds."

Baldy grabbed Zach's arms, marched to 408, the door already open, and shoved him inside.

No Keera. Three doors led off the main room. One closed.

"Lift arms," Baldy growled, releasing him.

Zach obeyed.

A fist slammed into his ribs. He collapsed to all fours, pain stealing his breath. Another blow, fast and low, caught his temple.

The world vanished.

Keera opened her eyes. Morning light seeped through curtains.

Chains rattled. Her wrists. Ankles.

It came rushing back—the motel, the kidnapping, the damn drink that had blocked her powers. The Russians didn't know how effective they'd been.

No Zach. Not yet. Had he found a psychic? Or gone the

straight route—police, caution, avoidance of the "woo-woo," as he called it?

The light grew stronger. Then, something formed on the curtain. A vision.

A sign on a grassy embankment. Quest Apartments.

Across the road: Zach in his car—asleep.

Don't think—watch. Bardo's constant guidance.

A new image appeared: red rock mountains rising above a winding road, a town nestled below. The smell of pine hit her.

The scene shifted—to a low house with a red gravel driveway.

Then: a highway sign. Two destinations. One blurred. The other—Sedona.

The vision vanished.

Why was Zach asleep? Why hadn't he called the police? No time to unravel it. He was close. That was enough.

Sedona. The name stirred something. A spiritual center in Arizona. A long way from here.

The door opened. Semyon entered with four pills and a glass of water. Moved like a man nursing a hangover.

He removed one wrist chain, sat her up, and ripped the tape from her mouth like he enjoyed it. She didn't scream.

"You take now," he said.

She turned the tablets in her palm. The V-logo. Valium.

She'd taken them once before—wisdom teeth. Didn't knock you out, just made you dull and slow. She swallowed them.

"I need the bathroom," she said.

He grunted, detached the other chain, and led her to the bathroom.

She slid the door closed. Waited. He didn't reopen it.

She took the soap square from the shower. Kneeling, she

wrote on the glass: *Sedona. AZ.*

She didn't know what it meant, but it was a message. If someone found it before they scrubbed the place, it might unravel the whole thing. She replaced the soap.

The door opened as she flushed. Semyon watched her wash her hands, then grabbed her wrist and marched her back. Rechained her.

His arm brushed her breast more than once. She showed no reaction. Did that register as encouragement? God, she hoped not.

Later, the front door opened. She didn't know how much later—Valium warped time. Her thoughts were sluggish, hunger growing.

The Russians must be out getting breakfast. That's why she got Valium, not knockout drops. This might be the pattern. Wake, feed, drug, repeat.

She needed intel. Anything. She had names. That might rattle them. Make them wonder who she really was. But she needed more if she was going to scare them.

Much later: voices. Loud. Urgent. No Zach. A thud—like a body hitting the floor. More talk, quieter now. Uncertainty. A decision or deadlock.

The door opened.

Semyon and Yuri entered. Semyon's face was a mess—blood, tissues stuffed in his nostrils. He didn't speak. Tore the tape from her mouth. They unchained her, zip-tied her wrists. She slid her feet into boots.

In the next room, the travel bags were packed and stacked. They were leaving.

The four gathered, tense as soldiers before a charge. Vronsky stood at the door, gun in hand.

"We take stairs to basement," He said to her. "No noise, no struggle, or people die. Okay?"

She nodded.

He peered into the hallway, then signaled them out. They moved fast. Internal fire stairs. Down.

She didn't touch the ground—lifted by the elbows between Yuri and Semyon, hands jammed in jacket pockets. Holding their guns, probably.

At the basement, they stopped. Vronsky slipped through the door marked "Parking." Gave the nod.

They moved through. A car beeped as it unlocked. Seconds later, she was in the back seat of an SUV beside Vronsky. Semyon rode up front. Yuri drove.

They paused at the gate. Swipe. Then up the ramp. At the curb, Yuri waited for a break in traffic then merged with the morning rush.

CHAPTER 9

Zach sat up slow and easy. He was jammed behind a couch like a crumpled sleeping bag. Every breath made his ribs complain. He pulled himself upright and surveyed the room. Empty vodka bottles on the coffee table. Food wrappers piled nearby. All the bedroom doors were open.

The birds had flown. The most precious one with them.

The bastards had dragged him behind the couch so Keera wouldn't see him. Keeping her confused—that was how they'd control her.

He entered the main bedroom. One king-size bed, disturbed covers on one side only. Keera's. The pillow was indented where she'd slept. He bent close and sniffed. Her scent. A single black hair curled on the cotton.

She had been here. So close. Now, gone again.

He checked the kitchen—dirty dishes, smeared tumblers stacked in the sink. A million fingerprints left by people who never expected to be caught.

The other bedroom held two rumpled single beds. No clues.

Keera probably hadn't been in there. But she'd have used the bathroom.

Brown tiles. Avocado basin. A glass shower screen beside a dry tub. No one had showered this morning.

He caught sight of himself in the mirror. Grimaced. Swelling around one eye, grazes beside it.

Toilet seat down. A tiny crumpled soap wrapper in the dish. Green soap bar next to it—mashed at one corner, but unused. Unwrapped and not used. People in a hurry.

He spent another ten minutes checking drawers and closets, but found nothing useful.

Downstairs, the concierge was sorting mail in the lobby.

"What happened to the Russians in 408?" Zach asked.

The Sikh concierge looked up. "What is wrong? Are they not opening the door?" His eyes widened as he saw Zach's face.

"The door's open. But they've gone. I was supposed to meet them this morning."

"Gone?" The concierge dropped the mail on a table and hurried to the elevator.

They rode up together. "My goodness," he muttered, stepping into the apartment. "They never said they would leave early."

"Did they owe money?"

"Oh no. Paid one week in advance." He looked around. "Not so messy, actually. Three men can be untidy without a woman."

"They didn't have a woman with them? I was meeting one here."

The concierge shot him a look. "This is a respectable building. No women like that here."

"That's not what I meant," Zach said quickly. "It was a business meeting."

"Yes, yes." He didn't believe him.

The concierge inspected the bathroom. "Not too bad. What's this mess on the glass?"

Zach followed. A smeared word had been written at the base of the shower screen in soap flakes. He knelt. Keera's handwriting. Faint but legible: *Sedona AZ.*

"You know what it means?" the concierge asked.

"Some Russian memo," Zach said, reaching for his phone. Nothing. He patted his pockets. No wallet. No keys.

"What are you doing?" the concierge asked, suspicious.

"My stuff's gone. Phone, money, keys." He checked behind the couch. Nothing.

"Why look there?" the concierge said. "Why not keep things in pockets like everyone else? And you said you weren't even here."

"I was. Briefly."

"And your colleagues hit you? What kind of business meeting was this?"

"It didn't go as planned."

"Yes, well." The concierge had had enough. "I must prepare for the next tenant." He bustled Zach out.

Outside, Zach paused think. Russians. The new mafia. The worst. He'd read the reports. Their tactics made the old Italian mob look like schoolyard bullies. The traditional codes were gone. The Russians didn't even spare families from the violence.

And they had Keera. All he had was *Sedona AZ.*

What was it? A destination? A clue? A warning? Had Keera left it for him deliberately? Maybe her captors slipped, or someone whispered it to her. Didn't matter. It was all he had.

His car was untouched. No tickets. He crouched at the driver's door, felt under the bodywork, and retrieved a black magnetic case. Inside: a spare car key and his apartment key. Ever since locking himself out once, he kept it there—just in case.

Inside the car, he pulled his old phone from the glove box. Popped in a prepaid SIM, ran the engine, and set it charging. Ten fumbling minutes later, it was live.

He called the *Post*. "Get me Danielle Kruger."

"Danny, it's Zach. I need a flight to Sedona, Arizona. Can you book it?"

Danny, 24 going on 50, was the department gatekeeper—travel vouchers, expense forms, pursed lips.

"Got the authorization slip?" she asked. "I don't see anything here."

"No. I just got on to a story and need to be there ASAP. Driving to O'Hare now. Text me the booking number. And I'll need a rental—base model's fine."

"Get Edwina's approval to me as soon as," she said, and hung up.

Booking a flight without approval would cause grief later. Even paying it back wouldn't help if there was no story. It could look like fraud.

Didn't matter. If he didn't find Keera, job security wouldn't be his biggest problem. Not by a long shot.

He dialed his old phone company, still in his contacts. Spoke to someone named Shaun—probably in Bangalore.

"I need you to kill my current phone and reactivate this number."

"Yes, sir," Shaun said in careful English. "May take a few hours."

"I need it faster. It's urgent."

"I will ask my manager to expedite, sir."

Zach tossed the phone on the passenger seat and merged onto the freeway.

O'Hare was fifty minutes away. His phone rang after fifteen. Danny.

"You're on US Airways to Flagstaff," she said. "No direct flight to Sedona. Leaves at two. You missed the morning runs."

"Fuck," he muttered, slamming the wheel. The Mustang lurched. "That's four hours away."

"Arrival's around eight. Sedona's an hour's drive from there. Rental's booked—base model. Nothing else is reimbursed." Click.

He pulled off the freeway to find a branch of his bank. Got handed a replacement debit card.

"You can't use this on the internet," the bank clerk said. "You have to wait for the proper card to arrive by post."

He withdrew some cash immediatelty, and strode back to his car. Seven hours flying. An hour of driving. A full day gone—and he'd barely started.

And what was he going to do in Sedona?

Wait. Keera had left one clue. She'd leave another. She had to. And this time, he'd be ready. No more improvising.

Arizona had loose gun laws. No permits needed. A few gray areas on concealment, but open carry was fine. He pictured himself holding a pistol. Facing her captors. Aimed and ready. Except it wasn't real.bHe'd never fired a weapon. Not since a BB gun at sixteen. He wasn't a killer. Couldn't even bluff it.

But the Russians wouldn't know that. They were armed. If he drew, they'd assume intent—and shoot to kill.

He slouched lower in his seat. Traffic swept him along. The signs for O'Hare appeared ahead.

His brain raced with possibilities and smacked into dead ends. Tell the cops when he got there? Not likely. Sedona was a magnet for the spiritual crowd—shamans, yogis, seekers drawn by red rock formations and sacred whispers.

But cops were still cops. Everywhere. Cynical. Suspicious. Smug. He'd get nothing from them.

His phone pinged. Danny's text with the booking.

He was good to go. With one plan—find Keera. At any cost.

CHAPTER 10

How did this come to be? Vronsky wondered as they drove down 55th. Morning rush hour had stalled traffic in the opposite direction, but they were moving fast enough to flush out a tail—if one was there.

How had the boyfriend found the girl? Was he working alone? Where was his backup? None of it made sense. His neck and shoulders ached from tension, from expecting a bullet through the window at any moment.

He pulled the boyfriend's things from his jacket, switched off the phone to kill any GPS tracker, and examined the keys.

"We've got an apartment key, looks like," he said. Then pulled the ID from the wallet. "And an address." He studied the driver's license, then swiveled to glance out the rear window. Pointless. If professionals were tracking them, he'd never know.

"If it's real, I'll wait at his place," Semyon said from the front seat. He pulled a wad of tissue from his nostril and checked it.

"What are you looking for?" Yuri asked. "It's got blood on it—just like you expected."

Semyon didn't reply. He pressed a clean tissue to his nose, then checked for swelling. None. He flipped the sunshade and peered into the mirror. A cut marked the tip of his nose, blood crusted on his upper lip and chin. He wiped it away.

"Don't annoy him," Vronsky said. "He recognized the boyfriend's car from two nights ago. Saved us a load of trouble."

"Lucky I didn't shoot through the door when you pounded on it," Yuri muttered. "Wasn't the knock signal we agreed on. Only thing saved him was you calling out."

"There was no time. I didn't know where the boyfriend was headed, or who with. We had to move fast."

"He knew to stop at the fourth floor," Semyon said. "How'd he know that?"

"This whole thing is very peculiar," Vronsky muttered.

"And I got no breakfast," Yuri grumbled, switching lanes with the traffic flow.

"We needed to check on him," Vronsky said. "Drive for another half hour, then stop at a mall. You'll get breakfast then." How did the FSB hire such a woman?

"And after that?"

"I'll have new instructions."

What those would be, he didn't know. No time to debrief after they dragged the girl from the motel. They could already be under surveillance. Might have been for days.

"You see the same car behind us?" he asked Yuri.

"If I did, I'd say so." Yuri checked the mirror again, then shifted his irritation toward Semyon. "Still don't get how you're the one bleeding, and the boyfriend's untouched."

"He was quick," Vronsky said.

"He had tools. You had a gun, Semyon. And you lost? Must've

had special powers."

"I didn't lose," Semyon snapped. "I caught him. Showed him consequences."

"He got in a lucky hit," Vronsky said. "Not the right place for gunplay."

He turned to Keera. She sat still, hands in her lap, eyes closed. The Valium would keep her docile for hours.

"What's your boyfriend's occupation?" he asked in English.

She stared at the driver's license in his hand. The keys in the other. "What's your interest in him?" she said, voice sluggish, like it was leaking from her.

"I ask. You answer. We saw him visit, but didn't know his job. It wasn't important before. It is now."

"What did you do to him?"

Still defiant. Even under sedation, she had backbone. Most hostages folded quickly—fear, shock. But she challenged him. Ignored her own danger. Spoke like an equal.

"He came to see you this morning," he said.

Her eyes opened. "What did you do to him?"

"Nothing serious. But we had to leave fast."

She slumped back. Glanced at Semyon. "Is that why he's bleeding? There was a fight? Zach got away?"

She didn't seem interested in the answer. That was the drug talking. Vronsky ignored her questions.

"The puzzle is how he found you."

"I wished for him to come and save me. And he did."

He considered slapping her. Later, maybe. "What's his job?"

"He's a journalist."

"He must be more than that. Works for a government agency."

"If he does, he never told me." She looked him squarely in the eyes. "This makes your situation complicated, doesn't it?"

"It complicates yours more. Your boyfriend isn't who he seems. Maybe you aren't either."

"Can you clarify that?" she said. "I'm in no condition to unravel complexities."

"I think the journalist job is a cover. He's with you for protection. And he failed."

She gave a faint smile. "I'm that important? I'm an assistant professor."

"Academics don't have the means to summon help like you did."

She turned to the window, ending the exchange. Too calm. The sedative had worked too well. He needed her afraid. Talkative. That would come later. He'd press her harder.

He switched to Russian. "Drop me at the mall, Yuri. I need to contact our man. Circle until I call."

Yuri frowned at him in the rearview. "We should stay together to plan. Call now."

"Normally, yes. But I have to speak in English, and she understands that."

"You'll bring back breakfast? American one?"

"First-class American. Donuts and coffee."

Yuri pulled into the shopping mall ten minutes later. Vronsky stepped out. Held the door as Semyon slid into the back.

"Don't touch her," he said. "We may have to bargain with people more powerful than I thought."

"She's begging me to touch her. With her eyes," Semyon said.

"Nobody ever begged you for anything, Semyon, except to leave."

Vronsky watched the car drive off, then headed inside.

Ten minutes later, coffee in hand, he dialed.

"This better not be a problem," said the Texan.

"It is. A serious one."

"Explain."

"Her boyfriend found us. We don't know how. She probably doesn't either. We neutralized him, got his ID, but couldn't stay for questioning. What now?"

"How could he find her unless y'all were incompetent?"

"Impossible. We were careful. Maybe she has a microchip."

"Those don't work long-distance. Forget it. Someone's watching her. That's bad. Very bad."

"If it's government—FBI, CIA—they could be following us now. If the team's big enough, we wouldn't know."

"Exactly. Something else is going on. I need to think."

"What do we do while you're thinking?"

Thirty seconds of silence. Then: "Go to Aurora Airport. Private jet from Leonard Air Services will take you to a safe house. Let's see if they can follow that. I'll have an answer then."

The line went dead.

This changed everything. The project might be dumped, delayed, restructured. More time in the U.S. More time away from Sasha.

Dumb kid. Twenty-five. Already messing with the heroin they were importing from Afghanistan.

Vronsky found out right before leaving.

"Father, I'm not an idiot from the backstreets. I know what I'm doing."

"The hell you do," Vronsky said. "I've seen strong men fall to that shit. Turned to shadows. The ones who lived."

Sasha had shrugged and kissed him goodbye. The words hadn't landed.

Now Vronsky tried Sasha's phone. Six p.m. there. Straight to voicemail.

Hearing his son's voice—confident, casual—brought back the boy he used to be. Before the rebellion. Before his mother left.

At the beep, Vronsky said, "It's me. Hope you're well. I'll call tomorrow."

He meant: Stay the hell away from that shit. He called Yuri. "Pick me up. Same spot. Dunkin' or Krispy Kreme?"

Yuri pulled up ten minutes later. Vronsky handed him a tray of coffees and a box of donuts, then climbed in beside Keera and Semyon.

"Aurora Airport," he said.

Yuri shoved a donut in his mouth, tapped the GPS, and pulled away.

"We going home?" he asked in Russian.

"We're meeting the paymaster. Situation's changed. New plan coming."

He pointed to the box. "Leave the Rocky Road for me."

CHAPTER 11

T he Toyota glided west and reached Aurora Municipal Airport half an hour later. Vronsky strained to puzzle out the morning's events and failed. One thing was clear: if the rescue crew had found the apartment, they likely had the means to track them—at least to the airport. They wouldn't be expecting a waiting plane. Flint was right about that.

"You think we have a bug in the car?" Yuri asked as they approached a boom gate.

A uniformed guard stepped out of a booth, checked the license plate, nodded once, and raised the barrier. Yuri drove through.

"A bug, no," Vronsky said. "That takes time. A tracker? Much easier. It would explain how the boyfriend found us." He pointed to a private jet marked with the Leonard Air Services logo. Yuri pulled up alongside.

A mechanic inspected the plane. The pilot, in uniform and cap, waited by the stairs.

Semyon drew a gun and ran the barrel down Keera's thigh. She flinched and shifted away.

Vronsky got out and approached the pilot. "We leave right away, yes?"

"That's the instruction."

"Good. We're boarding now."

Vronsky returned to the car and climbed in beside Keera. He took a penknife from his pocket and sliced through her wrist ties.

"This is what will happen," he said. "You walk to the plane. Straight to the back. No talking. No looking at anyone. If you do, Semyon shoots you in the spine. You'll spend life in a wheelchair. We can come get you again anytime. Everyone who's seen us here—dead. Understand?"

She rubbed her wrists, eyes locked on his. She nodded slowly.

Semyon handed her a cap and sunglasses. "Put on. All hair under."

She bunched her hair up under the cap. The Oakleys were too large but stayed on.

Vronsky climbed out and held the door as she stepped down, legs shaky. He caught her arm, steadied her.

Inside, the aircraft was a flying lounge. Four cream leather seats faced each other with wood-paneled tables between them. Further back, narrow single seats flanked either side.

Vronsky led her to a rear seat. "Bathroom behind you. Food comes soon."

The aircraft door whined shut. A flight attendant secured the lever and moved forward.

"Vodka and nuts," Vronsky told her. "One bottle, three glasses. The lady gets soda and a ham sandwich. Then we need privacy."

"After takeoff. Seat belts, please." She waited for clicks, then vanished behind the curtain.

"Nice ass," Semyon muttered. "Not so much the face."

The attendant returned with an envelope and handed it to Vronsky. The jet taxied, lifted smooth and steady. Minutes later, it banked south and climbed. Vronsky slit the envelope and removed a single sheet. containing a single printed line: 1027 Coyote Way, Sedona. Car waiting at airport.

He passed it to Yuri.

"Sedona? Where's that?"

"Arizona. The Wild West."

The vodka arrived. Semyon propped up a table, cracked the bottle, and poured for everybody.

"*Za vashe zdorovie*," Vronsky toasted. They drank in one.

The attendant brought Keera's sandwich and Coke. Vronsky stopped her. "I'll give them to her. She's not well." He handed the tray to Yuri.

"She's sleeping again," Yuri said when he returned.

They drank in silence, dozing in turns. An hour later, Semyon spoke.

"This changes the money."

Vronsky opened one eye. Semyon hadn't been sleeping—he'd been calculating.

"That depends on what new instructions we get," Vronsky said.

"It doesn't matter. We agreed on a price for one job. Now the job's changed. New price."

Not a bigger cut—he wanted a bigger pie.

"Maybe," Vronsky allowed. "If the situation gets more complex."

"I don't like 'maybe,'" Semyon said. "I like 'definite.'"

"You have a direct nature, Semyon. But sometimes it's best to wait before making demands."

Semyon wasn't wrong. But best not to agree too fast.

Yuri leaned forward. "Everything's changed. Before, we held the girl for a short time, then released—or killed—her. Now we've got the boyfriend problem. Do we kill him? That's more risk. That's more money. Semyon's right."

Yuri siding with Semyon? That was new. Was it the jet? The vodka? The scent of higher stakes?

"How much are we talking?" Vronsky asked.

Yuri hesitated.

"Double the fee for the girl," Semyon said. "And a hundred thousand if we kill the boyfriend and he disappears forever."

Vronsky drained his glass. Double? Two million for a hostage video? Another hundred grand for a body?

Flint wouldn't go for it. The man wasn't stupid.

"Your proposal has merit," Vronsky said carefully. "I'll see what our employer says."

"You tell him," Semyon said, "if he wants to use her, new terms apply."

Vronsky remembered Flint's voice—tight with panic—after hearing about the boyfriend. He was sure to be considering new options by now. Any more in this chapter

"Of course," Yuri added. "If there's no extra money, we have a business opportunity. She's worth a million to him? She's worth at least that to someone else."

"To whom?" Vronsky asked.

"I don't know. But our ex-employer will tell us. Won't he,

Semyon?"

Keera woke to the plane slicing through clouds. No land visible.

The sandwich lay untouched in front of her. She tore open the wrapper and slipped out the ham. Took a small bite of the rest of it.

The Valium's edge had dulled. It would linger for hours, but its peak had passed. Most people could shrug it off. Not her. Drugs, alcohol—anything that dulled the senses—wrecked her intuition. She'd known that since she was a teen. A kind of karmic penalty for being too psychically open.

She sipped the Coke and made a face. Tried to picture Zach, tried for a flash, a vision. Nothing. "Damn that shit they gave me."

She turned to logic—what other people used. Zach had found her. Been caught. But Vronsky said he wasn't dead—and she believed him.

The thuds she'd heard—those had to be Zach. But no fight noises, no shouting. They'd subdued him fast and hidden him.

He had to be in the apartment. Would he search for clues? Of course. Would he find the Sedona message? He'd better.

The plane began to descend. She saw mountains—red-brown ridges, tree-strewn slopes. Canyons cut through them. Then, ahead, an airport perched on a mesa.

The jet banked hard. Semyon, now beside her, swore and gripped the armrest.

The landing was smooth, and they taxied to a set of hangars. A black SUV waited nearby, windows tinted darker than the paint. The stairs eased down.

Yuri went first. Semyon waved Keera forward. She shuffled out. The pilot and crew stayed onboard.

Vronsky opened the SUV's rear door. Semyon pushed her in.

"This is for you," Vronsky said, handing her a black cloth bag. "Put it over your head."

She hesitated. Semyon raised his hand. She removed her cap and glasses and pulled the bag on. It smelled of laundry detergent.

The drive was ten minutes. Or twenty. She couldn't tell.When they stopped, hands yanked her out.

Into a house—cool from the hum of an air conditioner—down a hall, up stairs, a turn. A lock clicked. A heavy tread moved around the room. Tiles. A bathroom?

Then silence. Breathing near. Close. She tensed. A hand slid down the front of her dress. She slapped it away. Another hand gripped her buttocks, hard. She gasped.

Kicked out blindly, but connected with nothing. Fingers crushed her throat as the bag was ripped off her head.

Semyon grinned. "Later," he said. "We have time."

He closed the door behind him. The lock clicked. She exhaled. So much for hope.

There would be no clean exchange. No father's deal. No professional handover. Semyon would insist on "savoring the wares." To him, she was nothing but a desirable set of body parts. His to use, abuse and discard like a broken doll.

CHAPTER 12

The black Mercedes rolled up to the front door. The engine cut out. Headlights dimmed. Vronsky stood under the porch light as Flint stepped from the rear seat.

Same presence as before—controlled, commanding. Short, military hair. A suit from another tax bracket. His driver, thickset and crammed into a chauffeur's outfit, stayed behind him.

Flint strode over, snapping, "Unbelievable mess this is," brushing past and entering the house.

In the living room, Vronsky opened a low cabinet, revealing bottles.

"Unnecessary," Flint said. "This won't take long." He checked Semyon by the window, then turned back.

Vronsky poured vodka anyway, catching Flint's glare. Let him learn who's in charge now.

"Is the girl here?" Flint asked. "Safe, unhurt?"

"Upstairs. Looks like she's on a holiday."

"At least something went right. What's she like? Obedient?

Difficult?"

Semyon said, "Tasty tits. Mouth made for sex."

Flint blinked.

Vronsky ignored the comment. "Smart. Smart enough to be cautious. But not scared. Like she knows something we don't."

"I'll tell you what," Flint said. "Once we sent the image to the target, we were done. He'd know we could take his kid anytime. As soon as the contract was locked down, she'd be freed. The question is—and it's a big one—who the hell is this guy who screwed everything up?"

The driver stood in the doorway, arms folded.

"She says he's her boyfriend. Our intel backs that up," Vronsky said. "But love alone doesn't locate someone in hiding."

"Where's he from?"

"Does it matter? It's government. Has to be. Only they have that kind of reach. Which means—"

"Which means what?"

"They've been watching her for a while. And now they're watching us."

"Tracking device?" Flint paced.

"Could be on our car."

"Exactly." Flint's jaw tensed. "They're watching already, and I'm just a contractor bidding for work. Why do I matter?"

"You'd know better than me. But they're not acting, just watching. Maybe we've crossed into an op they care more about."

"Did you get a name off her?"

"We got the boyfriend. Took his ID. Zachary Bones. Journalist. She confirmed it. Too dopey for more questioning. We'll let the pills wear off."

Flint turned to the driver. "Call the office. Run a check on

Zachary Bones. Journalist, Chicago."

The driver pulled out a phone, murmured instructions, eyes still fixed on Semyon.

"What'd you do to him?"

"You said no cops. We couldn't shoot him and leave him there. Just gave him a lesson."

Flint nodded. "Got her phone?"

Vronsky handed it over. Flint played the clip, then passed it to his driver.

"One take?"

"We've done video before. There are rules—emotion must read true."

The driver's phone trilled. He answered, then passed it to Flint.

"Zachary Bones. *Chicago Post.* Six months."

"He's no journalist," Vronsky said. "He handled Semyon and me without weapons. Like a SEAL. Fit. Fast. Could've called backup and ended us right there. But didn't. Means no interest in us—only the girl."

"That's the problem." Flint rubbed his chin. "She has protection. If they knew where she was before, they might know now. Whole thing stinks. I'm pulling the plug."

Vronsky shrugged. "Your call. We agreed on a fee. We took the girl, held her like you asked. If the job ends early, we still expect full payment."

"A million? For grabbing a girl and letting her go? No return for me?" Flint scoffed. "Keep the two-fifty starter. Take her to Vegas, release her. Make sure she can't trace this place. Done deal."

Vronsky drained his vodka and replaced the glass on the cabinet. "Call it what you like. We want the full amount."

The driver shifted, slid his phone into his pocket, unbuttoned his jacket.

"You're nuts, Russkie." Flint laughed tightly. "Take the money. You've done well. *Hasta la vista,* but we'll work again someday."

"No promises," Vronsky said. "Money. That's the only agreement."

Flint shook his head. "It's over. Sure as hell, it's over."

A gunshot cracked the air. The driver jerked, then slid down the doorframe.

Yuri stood in the doorway, gun raised.

"Nothing's over," Vronsky said. His ears rang. What was Yuri doing? The driver had reached for something—but the kill was premature.

"What the hell?" Flint stared at the body, then at Yuri. "Think wasting my guy changes anything? The deal is OFF. O-F-F. Off." He gestured at the corpse. "This just made it worse."

To Vronsky's surprise, there was no panic in him. Just irritation.

"Governments aren't all-powerful," Vronsky said. "They can't stop money moving between friends. We want full payment."

He barked in Russian, "Check the car. There might be money."

Semyon stepped over the body and left.

"Just coffee money," Flint muttered.

Vronsky raised an eyebrow. "You understand Russian? Then I'll say it in English. Hiring us—coffee money for you too, I think. But we don't work for promises. My men came for a million. I need my word to mean something."

Flint looked at Yuri, now with his gun lowered. "Here's what you need to understand. There's something bigger going on. If I keep pushing, men in dark suits show up. Tax audits. Immigration raids. You get it? I fold and play nice. You? You get erased."

"So why the interest in the girl?"

"Beats me. And I don't care anymore. No money in this."

He reached into his driver's jacket, pulled out the girl's phone. "Keep the cash. We'll work again. Promise."

"The phone stays."

Flint's expression tightened. "You want it? It's useless now. No demands coming."

"Maybe not from you. But we're invested in this case."

"You're insane. This isn't Moscow. You're not shaking down oligarchs in Arbat Street. You're being watched—and you want to go solo?"

Vronsky pointed upward. "We have the girl. The target must have money."

"Oh, I see where this is going. I give you a name and address, and you handle it?"

"We don't have your deadlines. Makes it easier. Simple trade: one girl, one million. Maybe more."

"No chance. He's too connected. Layers upon layers. You'd never reach him."

"It was supposed to be easy for you."

"My plan was easy," Flint snapped. "No ransom crap. Just a normal contract. No one had to know. You're using Stone Age methods—they don't work here."

"We'll see. Write his email."

Flint did nothing.

"Then you go free."

"I'm already free." Flint stepped to the cabinet, poured a

scotch, raised his glass. "Cheers."

"You think I'm joking?"

"You're not thinking. This stays quiet—that's the point. That's why you didn't kill Bones. Shoot me, and attention rains down. You'll be three potatoes in a corn basket. You get picked up —it's a death sentence."

Flint drank. "They say alcohol's a weakness. I think it makes me brave."

Semyon reappeared, holding an envelope.

"It doesn't have to be this way," Flint said. "You're short-sighted."

"Maybe. But we have standards. Cancel a contract without proper comp, there's a penalty. We're not religious, but some rules are sacred."

Vronsky nodded to Yuri.

One shot. Flint's head snapped. Blood sprayed. He crumpled. Vronsky rubbed his ears, reached for the envelope. He dumped it onto the table. Bundled cash. He riffled a stack.

"Another hundred grand. He thought we'd haggle. I might've —but he started too low."

Yuri holstered the gun. "Now what?"

"Why did you shoot the driver?" Vronsky asked.

"He was going for a gun. I thought we should make a statement."

Bože materi. "No more killing without my say," Vronsky said.

Yuri rolled his eyes. "So—what now?"

"We take the money and erase all traces. This is no longer private. The cops will come. If they find our prints, they'll match them to our airport records. We need time to leave the country clean."

Yuri stared at Flint. "We shouldn't have killed him. He'd have told us the target."

"Look at him. He was an operator. A pro in a place where law doesn't scare anyone. He wasn't some soft-bellied bureaucrat. He wouldn't have talked."

"We made a mistake," Vronsky said.

"What mistake?"

"We left him with nothing to live for."

His own mistake. Yuri's shot had thrown him off.

"So what now?"

"We ask the girl. She'll know the target. Likely a relative. A man. Parents, maybe. We'll find out."

"How do we get their money?" Yuri asked, more confident now. Guns had that effect.

"Same way. Cayman account, split into parcels, through Russia, then Kazakhstan. When it lands, you get your share."

"Then we release her?" Semyon asked.

"No. We move her. Then we end it. Best if her death isn't linked to this scene."

"Not so fast," Semyon said. "You don't waste a body like that."

Yuri turned to him. "And you don't act without agreement."

CHAPTER 13

Thirty minutes passed after Semyon left before Keera regained a measure of calm and surveyed her surroundings. Another bedroom, this one more luxurious. A king-size bed dominated it; mahogany doors opened into a closet that contained men's clothes. Mostly casual wear. A large window overlooked a few yards of lawn; past that, scrubby bushes dotted the desert. More mountains guarded the way west. No other house in sight. She inspected the window frame. Sealed shut.

Who had been here before? No other hostages. The clothes suggested a regular occupant. In the bathroom, white towels, and a white terrycloth bathrobe hung from a hook. She ached for a shower but didn't dare take one. Being naked anytime in front of Semyon would be interpreted as a distinct invitation for rough sex.

She removed her jacket and, leaning over the basin, washed as best she could without removing her dress. Fresh clothes would rejuvenate her, but they were as elusive as freedom. She replaced her jacket and sat on the bed. Eyes closed and hands un-clasped on her lap, she breathed deeply and was grateful when, even in this stressed environment, she slipped into a trance. She waited for something, anything to happen.

Don't look for specifics, Bardo had trained her. Allow yourself to see what others wish to show you. Nothing came. Nobody wanted to show her a thing. Or couldn't.

"Damn that shit they gave me," she said.

A gunshot made her jump. A second one froze her heart. She kept her eyes on the door. What's happening? No answer from Bardo. Not Zach, please say it's not Zach. She tried to stop her raging thoughts from crashing into one another. Calmed herself long enough to see the obvious. It couldn't be Zach; he couldn't have followed her so fast, even if he found her message right away.

No more shots. After ten minutes, she sat back on the bed and waited for footsteps. Something had gone wrong. Would they move her again? Out of the corner of her eye, she spotted a new shape alongside her.

A man standing.

She scrambled to her feet and backed away.

"You see me, right?" he said.

She could see some of him. Head, shoulders and his right arm. The rest of him wasn't there. Just a gap between the visible parts and the floor.

"You see me or not?" he barked.

He showed no fear, his manner forthright, as if he was used

to asking questions and getting answers. He wore a dark suit, one visible arm appeared to be folded over his other invisible one.

"I see you," she said. The newly dead, in her experience, were more cautious, more confused about their new state. He was different.

"Well, *they* can't. So what happens now?"

He was referring to the Russians, she guessed. "You go to the light."

"I don't see no goddamn light. I can't believe those apes shot me. They screwed everything up; they're dumber than dirt. I smacked the hairy one in the face after the little one killed me, but he didn't notice."

"He's not aware of you. You can't touch him now."

He man held his right hand out, palm down, and looked at it while he flexed his fingers. "It feels normal, but I can see through it."

"Can you see all of you?" Keera asked.

"Of course. What sort of question is that?"

"I only see parts of you. I don't know why."

"That must be weird, eh?"

"Why did you die?"

"Because I hired fools."

It was him, the one responsible for her kidnapping. Fire erupted in her belly.

"You, you fucking slime," she yelled. "You had me taken,

had me doped up, had me brought here to spend my last moments with psychopaths. What other fucking horror have you planned?"

"Whoa, lady." He stepped back.

"What's your name?" she said.

"Bobby Flint." He stared at her closely. His energy powerful enough to drag her toward him, forcing her to pull back on it. An energy he didn't know how to use. Yet.

"Well, Bobby Flint, why don't you fuck off to the light and leave me alone."

"Don't care about no light. I got unfinished business."

"You want to stick around and see how I get to join you on that side? When I pass over, you're going to need a real fast rebirth to escape me. And even then I'll follow you and torment you forever."

He held up his only hand. "Wait, it wasn't personal. Just business."

"Just business?" The fire erupted again. "Just fucking business? You destroy my life, and it's just fucking business?"

"Okay, I admit it, it was a step too far."

She wanted to throttle him, but it wasn't possible. Wanted him gone, but he wasn't going. Wanted out of here, but... a thought flashed on her. Flint was a way out. Not for sure, but just maybe. She drew deep breaths, steadied her heart, doused the rage within.

"How is it you see me, and they can't?" he asked.

"I was made this way. They weren't."

He digested her answer. "You talk to dead people?"

She nodded, not trusting herself to stay calm if she spoke.

"All the time?"

"If they want me to. If I'm not busy trying to escape from kidnappers."

"See any others besides me lately?"

"You're the first of the day," she said, "and the worst."

He ignored her gibes. "You must have guides and shit. I've read about this. Seen that guy on television."

"Your question is?"

"Your guide. He tells you what others are thinking, right?"

"Sometimes."

Flint smiled, his outline brightening with pleasure. "There was no agency watching you, was there? Dead people tell you what's going on, don't you? Like I can now watch those Russkies and know everything they say in their lingo. I even get what they're thinking without them seeing me."

He was fast. Dead maybe ten minutes, and already he was calculating angles, solving puzzles. If she could control him, she might unsettle the Russians enough to free her.

"We snatched somebody who does this freaky message shit." Flint wide-eyed as he worked through the kidnapping scenario. "Who talks to the dead like Doctor Dolittle talked to the animals." He grinned as he reached a conclusion. "That's how you got your boyfriend to find you, isn't it? He's like you, another freak show."

"It's not a freak show," she said, impatient with his questions. "Once you've been dead a while longer, you'll figure it all out. There's more to being dead than just being dead."

"So you two talk anytime you want." Flint cocked his head. "So how come he came alone, and not with a posse of police?"

God, he was annoying. Could she work with him? "Why didn't my boyfriend contact the police?" she said.

"Guess."

"He must have a reason to avoid them."

"Guess again."

"This is not a time to play fucking games."

Flint looked over the room. "This was my bedroom. It's relaxing here. I'd come here most winters."

"And I'm so pleased for you; it's such a nice room. It's easy to see how enjoyable it would be to stay here if you could leave when you wanted. If you weren't expecting to die any minute."

He turned back to her. "You aren't dying that soon."

"What do you know?"

"Would you believe those crazies? They plan to ask money for you."

"Wasn't that what you were doing?"

He shook his head. "I was just using a little pressure to produce the right result."

A little pressure. That's all her kidnapping was to him—a

little pressure. She swallowed all the invective that rose in her throat. "It didn't work, did it? Now you should make amends."

Flint shrugged. "What can I do? What do I care? My interest in this complete business has expired. Like me. All I want is to screw those Russkies."

"I suppose it's worth trying," she said. "They can't kill you twice."

"Exactly. I'm still around. I haven't gone anywhere, have I? I'm not in heaven or hell. I feel the same, except I got no physical body. And I move through walls. I only had to think of you, and I was beside you. That's a plus for sure."

"What are you going to do now?"

"Damned if I know, but you can see and hear me, and that's a start."

"You're thinking of using me?" The bastard was dead, and already assuming he was the leader. "I heard two shots," she said, trying to take charge. "Anyone else dead?"

"They killed my driver too. They're animals. I'm gonna get 'em for that, too."

"You're not on the physical plane anymore. You have limited means here."

"Well, I've seen ghost movies. I know they move stuff, cause problems. I'll figure out how to do it, too, and then bam, I got 'em."

"It's not as easy as it looks."

"If it can be done, I'll do it." He clenched his teeth like he was trying already.

Keera could see thoughts of revenge burned in him and welded him to the past. His death hadn't affected his personality either. He was a driven man, the type who gets to his goal no matter what or where. Even after death.

Flint said, "I notice you ain't going nowhere. I'll see what I can do to those yokels now."

"No! Don't start stuff until…"

He faded from view, and she sat on the bed again. This is getting worse, she said to the floor.

Flint had figured out the first advantages of being in spirit. He had enough energy to move things, or mess with electricity. If there was an outburst of poltergeist activity, the Russians might get alarmed. Who knew how they would react? They might blame Flint, or her. If they decided she was psychic, they'd connect that to Zach finding her in Chicago. And then… she didn't want to take that thought further.

Flint could be an advantage to her, if she could control him, find a way for them to work together. Would he do it? She didn't know. She knew one thing: she was the only contact he had in the physical world.

He'd be back.

She hoped.

◆ ◆ ◆

"The bodies," Vronsky said. "Take them away and lose them."

Semyon and Yuri bent over Flint and his driver. Semyon

worked through the driver's pockets and found his gun in the holster.

"Automatic Colt," he said. "This guy's still fighting Vietnam war."

"Leave it," Vronsky instructed. "We don't want it linking us to these two."

Yuri fingered Flint's tie. "Nice silk, but too much contrast with paisley. It's meant to be a subtle blend of colors." He didn't inspect the brain splatter on the cabinet.

From the kitchen, Semyon brought large garbage bags and yards of electrical extension cords. He wrapped and knotted, and when he had finished, two big black parcels lay on the floor.

They maneuvered Flint's body into the Mercedes trunk, and the driver's into the rear. Yuri fastened a seatbelt around the torso. "I don't want him flying into front if I have to brake quickly."

"That'd wrinkle your collar, eh?" Semyon said and slid behind the wheel of the SUV, waiting for Yuri to lead off.

"There's a road that leads further into desert west of here," Yuri said from the Mercedes, pointing to the GPS display. "We'll go there and drive car off road a few hundred meters. Dump it behind trees."

"A simple plan, a good plan, Yuri," Vronsky said, not bothering to look at the screen. "Bring back food."

Yuri led the two cars out, both sets of brake lights flashing at the end of the driveway before dimming and diminishing as they sped away.

Inside, Vronsky drained his vodka and placed the glass on the coffee table. He gathered up the two wallets and was fingering the contents when he stopped.

The glass was moving.

Slid an inch, stuttered to a halt, regained speed, enough to glide across the table, and fall off the edge.

Yuri led them north, checked the GPS for any turnoff. House-lights became fewer, and a couple of minutes later he turned left, onto a dirt track. He slowed after another mile and stopped, the SUV close behind him. He walked to the side of the road and kicked at the rocky shoulder. Satisfied, he returned to the Merce-des, drove on, and while traveling at thirty mph, wrenched the wheel to the right.

The big car, built for high-speed autobahns, struggled with Arizona desert. Rear wheels churned and spun through the sand, trying to find a grip. The task was too great, and after fifty yards it slewed to a halt. He used a handkerchief to wipe the steering wheel and the seat belt buckles. As an afterthought, he flipped open the glove box.

The SUV had stayed on the dirt track, and Semyon turned it around. When Yuri climbed in beside him, he showed the hand-gun he'd found. "Glock. Full clip."

"The 17?"

"The 19. Light, but still ugly."

"Good weapons," Semyon said, turning the SUV back toward

Sedona. "Never jam."

Yuri opened the glove box in front of him and dropped the weapon inside. "Do you think we can get good pastrami on rye?"

Semyon didn't answer until they paused at the road junction. "You were stupid to shoot driver."

"You've been thinking about it all this time?" What nutty idea did the goon have now?

"It was like, bang, man dead. No way left to put extra pressure on Flint." He turned the car towards the town.

"How would you have done it? The driver was reaching for his weapon."

"Grabbed his wrist and broken his face. Dragged him around in front of Flint and said 'Watch this' and snapped his neck. Mr. Texas would have told us everything. He'd still be talking while we were trying to sleep. You gave us no chance to scare crap out of him."

"I forgot, you're such a Superman. The rest of us have to rely on modern equipment." And fast thinking. Something Semyon wouldn't do, couldn't do.

"You said, on plane, that I could squeeze Texas to give us anything we wanted. Then you go with gun. And I had to carry carcass out." Semyon slowed as they entered Sedona. "You better stick to airline schedules and motel bookings. From now on, keep your face in a fashion magazine while real work is carried out. By me. Like we planned."

"I'll respond as required," Yuri said. See if you can stop me.

CHAPTER 14

The guy at the Flagstaff Airport car rental counter had buttoned himself into a burgundy suit he must have hated.

"You staying someplace nice?" he asked, eyes flicking to Zach's face.

The bruises would be turning a fancy shade of purple by now. "Heading to Sedona. Haven't booked anywhere yet," Zach replied, signing where the form was marked.

"Beautiful place. I took one of those vortex tours last weekend." The guy accepted the form. "You know, where unseen earthly lines of power intersect and create uplifting energy channels. In this cute pink Jeep."

"You get uplifted?"

"Felt better the next day. Can't expect miracles overnight. Driver's license?"

He'd forgotten. The Russians had it now. "Uh, left it behind. I work for the *Chicago Post*—we use your company all the time. I've rented from you before. It should be on file."

The guy looked genuinely sorry. "I need to see a physical license, sir."

Zach didn't argue. The guy was just doing his job and had no authority to bend the rules. "Okay, my bad. Where can I get a cab?"

"Happy Stan might still be outside. Green Prius. He'll do right by you."

Do right by me? Like not stop halfway and demand more cash to finish the ride? He stepped outside and spotted the green Prius.

"Can you take me to Sedona?"

The driver was over sixty, with a Yosemite Sam mustache and a gut that could double as a food tray. Happy Stan gave him a lazy once-over. "Hundred bucks. In twenties. In advance. No funny shit on the way or I throw you off a cliff—and there's plenty to choose from."

"Do I look like trouble?"

"You look like you already had a dust-up today and might be itching for seconds. I can handle myself."

Zach touched his cheek—tender, a little scabby.

"Industrial accident. I'm very placid." He handed over five twenties. "Any good motel in town."

The Prius pulled away without a sound, switching to gas as it turned onto A89 south. Zach sat up front.

"How long will it take?"

"Under an hour. Unless you want the scenic tour."

"Is that faster?"

"Same route. I just slow down and open the windows."

A comedian. "Skip the tour. I'd rather marvel at my destination."

Happy Stan wasn't wrong about the view. Stark red mountains jutted skyward, ponderosa pines clustered at their feet. The sinking sun bathed the land in a God-level light show. The road switchbacked down through cliffs and drops—plenty of places to toss a passenger.

"You ever think about all the evil in the world?" Stan asked.

"That's a big topic," Zach said. "I'm too shallow to grasp it." Hint dropped. No luck.

"Used to be, expose corruption and the bastards got shamed out. Not now. They stay. Some even love the attention."

He looked over. "You notice that?"

The Prius drifted. Cliff edge loomed.

"Hey," Zach said. "Watch the road."

"I got it," Stan said, pulling back into lane. "Relax. I've driven this road for years."

"Let's keep it that way."

They rode in silence for ten minutes before Stan tried again.

"You don't look like a normal visitor, and you sure don't live here. I'd know. What brings you?"

Zach considered walking. Decided it was faster to humor him.

"I'm a reporter. Chasing a story."

"About what?"

"Can't say. Don't want to lose the scoop."

"You exposing corruption?" Stan getting excited.

"Maybe."

They rounded a bend. Adobe buildings appeared. A motel sign lit up on the left.

"That place," Zach said. "Drop me there."

Stan leaned over as Zach climbed out. "You nail those bastards. We the people only have truth and decency left."

"I'll try."

"Remember—evil can't exist in the glare of a spotlight."

"I've heard that too. Thanks for the ride."

Stan drove off. Zach looked at the motel but didn't go in. Though Sedona nights were known to be chilly, the air stayed warm as he strolled up the main street.

Vacationers packed the sidewalks. Vortex tours. Aura readings. Drumming meditation. Navajo jewelry. "Earth Wisdom" Jeep rides. Two kids squealed as they stuck their heads into a diner's mist spray mystery.

Zach crossed the street toward the corner market. – Monty's Mart, the sign said. Parked outside it, a black BMW SUV. And Baldy, the Russian he'd swatted that morning, getting out and stretching.

His heart screamed at him to charge the guy, to smash his face into the pavement; his head reminded him of the beating he wore the last time he listened to his heart. He ducked between two pickups, watching through their windows.

How the hell did Keera guide me to them like this? All the way to handshaking distance, almost. Was she with them? In the SUV?

Another man emerged. Thin and blond—one of the Russians from outside the fire door. Baldy clicked the key fob. The lights flashed and flashed again before they satisfied him. He pocketed the remote and they both moved inside Monty's.

Did two flashes mean locked or unlocked? It was easy to get it mixed up in a unfamiliar vehicle. Zach slipped down the row of parked cars. Opened the rear door. Interior light flashed on. Empty.

He opened the tailgate—also unlocked. Empty, with a fabric cover stretched over the space. He checked the street. No one close. He slid in, curled up like a suitcase, and pulled the hatch shut.

They took their time. He was fighting claustrophobia when the locks snapped shut... then open. Doors slammed. Bags hit the seats. The SUV rocked as they climbed in. The engine started. One of them muttered, a hand rummaged through plastic.

They pulled away.

Zach stayed still. Please, no one call me now. He tried reaching for his phone—stopped. His arm had pushed against the luggage cover. The driver might see it bulging in the mirror. He prayed instead. He'd had no luck lately. Maybe the tide was due.

Neither of the Russians spoke during the ride. Maybe some tension between them. They drove ten minutes before turning onto gravel. Light bled through seams in the cover. The SUV slowed, stopped.

More doors. More rustling. Then—click. Locks snapped shut. A door closed. He waited. No more sounds.

He groped for the trunk latch—couldn't find it. Mechanism shielded and impossible to figure out in the dark. He rolled up the luggage cover and crawled over the back seat. Tried the door handle.

Locked.

BMW double lock. No way out, even from inside.

He could kick out a window. Loud, especially with an activated shrieking alarm, but possible. But the gap would still be too small to exit quickly.

He was trapped. Delivered like packaged beef.

It was all wrong. He was out here. Keera in there. Neither

could reach the other.

The house was large. Front stretched at least thirty yards. The door was just steps away.

The exterior lights went out. Moonless, starless dark. No sound.

A faint glow behind a window blind—just enough to remind him he wasn't alone on the planet.

CHAPTER 15

The glass moved by itself," Vronsky said.

"Like, into your hand and then to your mouth?" Yuri said. "You've discovered a useful tool for mankind."

"I'm serious. I was checking wallets when it started sliding. No earthquake, no one bumped the table."

"Did it spill vodka?" Semyon asked, skeptical. "First drink or thirty-first?"

"I wasn't drunk." Vronsky pointed to the coffee table. "It moved—from there to there—then fell off."

They all stared at the table, then at the glass, now on its side on the carpet.

"Nobody touched it?" Semyon dropped the shopping bags, pulled out two bottles of Stolichnaya.

"Slid by itself. I wasn't even drinking then. Later, for sure."

"Heard about this kind of thing once," Yuri said. "In my village. Old babushka died, stuff in her house started moving. Her son lost his mind, left the place."

"Glasses moved?" Vronsky asked.

"No mention of glasses. But a broom flew across the room when he messed the place. Doors slammed at night—locked ones. Mornings, all the kitchen cupboards were wide open. I saw it myself. Hinges so rusty, no way they opened on their own."

Semyon grunted. "You think it was her ghost, whacking the son with the birch?"

"She was house-proud. He was a slob. She wanted him gone."

"You're more stupid than you sound. He made it up."

"Why? To become a laughingstock?"

"Needed an excuse to leave. Told everyone his mother's spirit drove him out, instead of looking like a disrespectful bastard."

"Nobody bought the house after. How smart was that?"

Yuri pointed to the glass. "If that moved on its own, we've got a spirit here."

"What I have," Semyon said, "is a hard-on for the girl upstairs. That's what concerns me."

"It's all you think about. That part of your brain must be worn out."

"As long as the most important part of my body works, I'll live."

"Enough." Vronsky cut in. The killings had given the little fusspot confidence. Was Yuri dumb enough to challenge Semyon? Dumb enough to push it? Semyon would twist his head off like a bottle cap.

"The glass moved for a reason. I want to know why."

"We're in a haunted house, that's why," Yuri said. "I've read about this."

"What normally happens?"

"Stuff moves, gets hidden. Footsteps at night. Whatever's

here wants attention. If it turns violent, it means it wants us gone."

"To hell with that," Semyon said. "I've got frozen food, sandwiches, crackers, cheese, pickles. How long are we staying here, anyway?"

"Who could the spirit be?" Vronsky asked. "One of the Americans?"

"Or the original owner. Maybe some Indian who hunted here."

"What crap are you reading?" Semyon opened the pickles.

"Books without naked women," Yuri said.

"Your loss."

"Can it harm us?" Vronsky asked.

"No. Spirits don't kill. We move on."

"Good. We won't be here long." But it was a problem. If a spirit could move a glass, what else could it move? If it was Flint...

"What now?" Yuri asked.

"Find out what the girl's father does, make text contact, and leave. Need to dump the phone soon."

Vronsky opened a cabinet, poured vodka into a fresh glass.

"The Americans—are they well hidden?"

"I did what I could. No spade. They're off-road. Won't be found before daylight."

Vronsky downed the drink, looked at the fallen glass again.

"Flint will be listed as missing soon. If this house is his, cops will check here. We need a new place."

"The girl," Semyon said. "Is she ready to cooperate?"

"Didn't ask. But she'll do what we say if her father's the target. To save him."

"Save him? New plan?"

"We tell her: if he doesn't pay, she dies, and he dies after. She'll cooperate. Her instinct's to resist. This'll change that."

"She has his number?"

"Of course. We film her again, send the image."

"We already have one."

"Too sweet. She didn't look scared enough. I'll reshoot. More drama."

"Why not fuck her on camera?" Semyon said.

Vronsky nodded. "If he doesn't pay, we escalate. He'll have 24 hours to deposit money. He'll think he gets her back."

"But we keep her?"

"Possibly. Depends how fast we can leave the country. No time for fun."

"When do we do it?"

"Now. Semyon, get her."

Keera heard car doors, the front door slam—then silence.

"Where are you, Flint? I need to know stuff."

"Someone mention my name?"

He was back, grinning like a kid. Most of him visible now—except his left leg.

"You look happy," she said. "I'm thrilled something nice is happening for you."

"I thought it'd be hard to move the glass. It wasn't. I concentrated—then let go. It slid across the table."

"Who saw it? You move anything else?"

"Vronsky saw. After the others returned, food covered the table. No space for more tricks. Tried the receipt—it slid under the sofa. Nobody noticed."

Thank God. If they thought she was psychic, they'd kill her.

"You've got energy, Flint. That's clear."

"That's what made me. Drive. Energy."

"It also got you killed."

"Shit happens."

"What was their reaction to the glass?"

"Vronsky—freaked. Big guy didn't believe it. Other one did." He brightened with a new thought. "You've been here longer than me. Can you show me how to move other stuff and shit?"

"I can't move stuff or other shit as you put it. Takes all my energy just to stay connected."

"I sense you don't like me."

"Why would I not like you?" she retorted. "You got me snatched, hurt my boyfriend, and plan to destroy my father. Apart from that, you're a peach."

"Okay, okay. So nobody's perfect. Every friendship has its sharp moments, right? But listen here, sister: you need me. You don't know what they propose for you, but I do."

"Tell me."

"They'll use you to get money. Then kill you. Maybe after some. sex play."

A gut-punch. She'd buried that fear. He'd unearthed it. "You have a plan to stop this?"

"Just found out. I'm good, but not that good." Flint looked around. "Aren't you supposed to have a guide or something?"

"My guide's here when I need him. Where's yours?"

"Didn't hire one."

"You've got one but maybe he found you irritating. Asked for reassignment."

"So funny. Where's your guide? Why hasn't he got you out of here?"

"Guides don't rescue. We steer our own lives."

"Your destiny looks catastrophic. I feel bad about getting you into this, and I want to help you. But if you're going to act all high and mighty, I withdraw my offer."

"You can withdraw it all the way up your ass for all I care."

She regretted the words instantly. He was uncontrollable and scratched her nerves every time he spoke. He wouldn't have been her first choice of an ally, but he was the only one on offer.

"I apologize for my remark," she said. "It was uncalled for."

"It's okay, little lady," Flint replied with relaxed magnanimity.

"Don't call me that."

"Okay, okay. No conniptions. What do you want?"

"I want to be free of those goons, and for the law to bring them to justice. What do you want?"

He raised a finger. "First, I want them to fail."

"Agreed."

"Second, I want them dead and in my world, so I can dish out my justice."

This man could do with some higher-level spirituality tuition.

"It's difficult to kill people when you're already dead yourself."

"That's where you come in."

"I'm not killing anyone. Plan B?"

"Let's mess with them and see what happens."

"How?"

"Not sure. But cavalry's arrived."

"What?"

"Your boyfriend. Outside."

"Zach?" She was astonished. And elated. "What's he doing?"

"Nothing." Flint laughed.

Why was this amusing?

"He's got himself locked in their car."

"How'd he do that? Were you there at the time? Did you—?"

"No. I followed them after they dumped the bodies in the desert. Stopped for groceries. Your Zach was there. He saw them, snuck into the trunk. They didn't see him. Locked the car. Now he's trapped."

"Why can't he get out?"

"Bimmer. Double locks. Needs the remote."

"Can he break a window?"

"Sure. Set off the alarm. Three armed killers rush out, unload on him while he's halfway through the glass. Great plan."

"Is he hurt?"

"Battered, not broken."

"Can you get him out?"

"I'm not advanced enough, remember? But I sat with him. Let him know he's not alone."

"And?"

"He can't see me. But he's got a plan."

She wanted to scream at Flint and sensed he knew it. He was dragging out the tale, to show who was in control. "What plan?" she asked with steely calm.

"A simple one. He's gonna wait until y'all return to the car, and then he's gonna, he's gonna... well, he's not sure."

She closed her eyes. A nightmare. She a prisoner, Zach trapped, Flint finding it hilarious, and the Russians primed to shoot Zach as soon as they saw him. Could it get any worse?

It could.

Semyon at the door. "You, come."

CHAPTER 16

Keera stepped around the bloodstains on the carpet and accepted the sandwich Yuri handed her. She sat on the couch, peeled away the roast beef, and bit into the rest.

Vronsky said, "You recall the film scene we shot before? The take was good, but we need a reshoot. Small problem with interpretation. Same lines, no new character to learn."

She kept chewing, silent. He saw the resistance in her face.

Yuri pulled her phone from his bag and passed it to Vronsky.

"Your performance last time was excellent," Vronsky said. "This time, we'd like to see the same energy and immersion." He flipped through her phone, opened the camera app, tapped the screen. The phone clicked like it had a shutter.

"Nice image," he said. "Crisp and clear. Perfect for capturing those special moments."

He switched to video mode, adjusted the angle, and slid the shopping bags and his glass to either end of the coffee table.

"Too much clutter in frame."

"Is this for Cannes?" Yuri asked. "Can we do this and go?"

"Sure. Get things together, book us a place."

Yuri pulled out his phone and left the room.

Semyon slouched in an armchair, eyes locked on her.

Vronsky raised the phone. "Ready, Miss? Your line is: 'I am being held. Please follow instructions in next text.'"

She paused mid-chew. "Who's getting this?"

"Your father."

"Why?"

"Makes the most sense."

"You think he's just available? Picks up calls from me, anytime?"

"He'll believe it's you. After he sees the pictures, he'll understand the situation."

"You're insane." She took another bite.

"All those who succeed are insane. Have you finished eating? We need to leave soon."

"I'd appreciate a drink. Is that possible?"

"No."

He looked at Semyon, who stood, walked over, and yanked the sandwich from her hands, flinging it across the room.

She wiped her mouth with the back of her hand.

Vronsky aimed the phone. "When I nod, say the line."

She slouched deeper into the couch. "Do I smile a little or cry a lot?"

"Look anxious. If not, Semyon will help."

The big man moved beside her. She tensed.

"Okay, let's roll," she said.

He hit record. She said, "Hi Dad, it's me. I'm in a jam here, as you can see, and these guys are going to ask you something. It's not a biggie, but can you do this without breaking any laws?"

Vronsky stopped recording. "What is 'biggie'?"

"An expression. Means 'not a big deal.'"

"Very polite, but not appropriate. Again. The line I gave you."
He hit record again.

"I am being held against my will. How are things with you?"

She said it flat. Semyon backhanded her face, once, then
again. She gasped, doubled over, hands covering her face.

He grabbed a fistful of hair, dragged her upright. "Say it properly. Now."

Vronsky held the camera steady.

"I am being held," she croaked. "Please do what they say."

"Excellent work," Vronsky said. "You'll get rave reviews." He
checked the playback. "It's good."

Semyon shoved her head aside. She buried her face back in
her hands.

Yuri returned. "You started without me. I'd have made her
look more vulnerable. There's a makeup kit in the master bedroom."

"She was fine," Vronsky said, biting back irritation. "Did you
book the motel?"

"Flagstaff. What does the text say?"

"I'm working on it. How about: 'Hi, Dad, here's an important
message to follow'? Then we send the video."

"'Hi Dad'? Too casual. Say, 'Dad, this is really urgent. Please
confirm by return text ASAP. Keera.'"

Vronsky nodded, typed the new message, then showed it to
Yuri.

"There are two l's in 'really' and one more 't' in 'text,'" Yuri
said.

Vronsky corrected it, attached the video.

"Miss Keera," he said, holding the phone to her. "No contact entry for him, but I know you know the number."

She lifted her head. Defiance all over her face.

"If you don't cooperate, we kill him after we kill you."

She hesitated, then took the phone, tapped in the number, and paused. Semyon shifted beside her. With a breath, she hit send and handed it back.

"Can I have my drink now, please?"

In the moment's pause, they heard a new sound.

A glass scraping on wood.

They all looked. Vronsky's glass slid across the table toward her—and stopped.

"God help us," Yuri said.

"What the hell?" Semyon picked up the glass, flipped it over, then pushed it with his fingers. It slid a few inches, stopped.

He dropped to his knees, checked under the table. "Nothing weird. No magnets."

"Glasses aren't magnetic," Yuri muttered. "Did you even go to school?"

"That's what happened last time," Vronsky said. He felt strangely vindicated.

Yuri pointed at Keera. "Maybe she's doing it."

"Never seen anything like this."

"Told you. Angry American spirits."

Semyon snorted. "They can try me. I'll rip their lungs out."

"Problem is, you can't touch them. But they can touch us."

"If all they can do is slide empty glasses, I'm not impressed."

Yuri looked at Vronsky's phone. "How long do we wait for a reply?"

"I haven't sent the video yet."

He found the last dialed number and sent the clip.

"I'll switch off soon so they can't track the phone. We'll check messages later."

"Could take days," Yuri said.

"No. Her father's not going anywhere. As soon as he sees the video, nothing else matters. We wait in a new place."

"Negotiating by text? That'll be tricky."

"What's tricky? We say: one million, twenty-four hours, in our bank. No more contact. If no money, we send death photos and go home."

"Not before I have her," Semyon said.

Keera lifted her head. She understood.

"Please," she said softly. "Can I have my drink now?"

CHAPTER 17

Twenty minutes in the car, and goosebumps pimpled Zach's arms. His cotton tee offered thin protection against the seeping chill. Again, he searched the door compartments and mesh pockets behind the front seats. Too dark to see, but his fingers told him the bad news: nothing warm.

His phone chimed, startling him. Loud enough to carry into the house? He yanked it out and stared at the screen. A text—from Keera.

Dad, this is really urgent and important. Please confirm you have this by return text ASAP. Keera.

What the hell?

He read the message again. And again, until the screen blanked out.

Was she free? If so, why wasn't she calling him? Why a text—to her father?

His phone chimed again. An attachment. He opened it.

Keera stared at the camera, calm but defiant. Behind her, a

man's torso appeared. A hand smashed across her head. Then again. Keera moaned, shielding her face. Another hand grabbed her hair, lifted her face to the camera. A voice muttered.

Then Keera, halting: "I am being held. Please do what they say."

The video ended.

Zach exhaled hard, his chest thudding. He kicked at the car door, then stopped. A shock might set off the alarm. No one emerged from the house. He tried to figure out what had happened. The kidnappers thought they'd sent the ransom demand to Keera's father. But she'd given them his number.

If he replied carefully, they'd keep believing it.

He typed: *Who is this?*

But instead of texting directly, he routed it through FlagMail, masking his identity. If the Russians saw no ID, they'd assume her father was cautious.

Another chime.

You like to see your daughter again. We need one million dollars in nominated account in 24 hours. Acknowledge now.

A million. They weren't amateurs. Keera's father probably had the cash. They'd done their research.

First priority: stop them hurting her again.

He composed a reply:

I have to know if she's fine. Send a new image within ten minutes.

But he had no way of knowing when the last image of her was taken. She only had to hold something they wouldn't have thought of. Something simple, a household object. A cup, a bowl, a glass. A glass was the easy choice. The Russians were probably knocking down their vodkas while they waited for his reply.

He added: *Please hold up a glass.* He hit send.

His adrenaline ebbed. The situation was terrible—but manageable. They'd eventually have to move. Sending ransom texts from one spot was stupid.

Now the cops. This they'd believe: video, text, proof. His thumbs hovered over the keypad. Stopped. And if police swarmed in, the Russians might panic. Keera was inside. With armed men. Unstable men.

He'd have to intercept them. Ambush them when they exited. And he needed warmth. Fast. Already shivering, he'd checked every compartment except one.

Zach leaned over the center console, reached for the glove box.

"A glass?" Vronsky shouted. "He wants a glass?"

"What the hell does that mean?" Yuri asked.

"We ask him for money, and he asks us for a glass?"

"It's a signal," Semyon muttered. "She asked for a drink, right?"

Yuri shrugged. "So what?"

Vronsky grabbed the glass from the table and shoved it at her.

"There's no water," Keera said.

"Just hold it up," he snapped, pointing her phone at her.

She lifted the empty glass with a flicker of a smile.

He snapped a few shots, checked them.

"All good. I send. Then we leave. Now. We've done killing here. Police will come."

Yuri swept food wrappers and glasses into a garbage bag, stuffed bottles into his backpack.

Vronsky sent the image. "We continue conversation in car." He yanked Keera upright.

Semyon led the way, scanning the yard. He reached the SUV, tossed the bags inside. Yuri clicked the remote. Lights blinked. Doors unlocked. He opened the back.

And froze.

A Glock. Pointed at his face.

"Well, this is awkward," said the boyfriend.

Vronsky lunged behind Keera, dragged her close, pulled his gun. Semyon dropped his bags, stepped back slowly.

Zach eased out of the car, Glock steady. Yuri had his own gun out now, trained on Zach.

"You call this Colombian standoff, no?" Vronsky said.

"Mexican," Yuri corrected. "Except it's not."

"How so?" Zach asked.

"Because you care more about girl than we care about him," Yuri said, gesturing at Semyon.

"Put your weapon down," Vronsky added. "It's best."

"Put yours down. Give me the girl," Zach replied. "We leave. You disappear."

Vronsky answered by raising his gun, aiming at Zach. "We could talk all night. But I count to three, then I shoot."

Zach hesitated. He couldn't risk it. If he fired, he might hit Keera.

He glanced at her. She nodded, quick and sharp.

"One," Vronsky said.

Zach dropped the gun.

Semyon scooped it up and smashed it into Zach's face. He stumbled, blood pouring from his nose. Keera cried out. Tried to break free.

"Keep moving," Vronsky snapped.

Semyon pointed the Glock at Zach.

"No," Vronsky ordered. "He comes with us. He explains."

Semyon kicked Zach's legs. He crumpled.

"Sit up. Hands on head," Semyon barked.

Zach obeyed. Semyon reached into the car, pulled out Zach's phone.

He scanned the screen. "Shit. Messages we sent went to him. Not her father."

Vronsky grabbed the phone. "The sneaky bitch."

"What now?" Yuri asked.

"We start over. We have girl and boyfriend. He tells us what we don't know."

"Should we resend the text to right number?" Yuri said. "We can move and wait for reply."

"We don't have the right number. Not sure which it is."

"We gambled," Yuri said. "We lost."

"Nothing else in car," Semyon added. "And how the hell did he get here? No jacket. No gun. Unless..."

"Friends nearby?" Yuri guessed.

"Then we're targets. Let's go."

Yuri shoved Keera into the front seat, zip-tied her wrist to the belt catch. Semyon dragged Zach up, wedged him between himself and Vronsky. Keera twisted to look back. Semyon struck her head. She turned forward. The SUV rolled out, headlights off. At the road, Yuri floored it. The doors locked with a clunk.

Vronsky swore at the dying battery on her phone. "She got charger?"

"We didn't bring her bag," Yuri said.

"Her phone's Samsung. We've got iPhones and Pixel."

"Buy new charger tomorrow."

"Too late. We lose time tonight."

"What's her dad's name?" Yuri asked.

"Miles. Nothing in contacts under that."

Vronsky switched to English. "Miss Keera, what's your father's first name?"

She mumbled. Semyon growled. She repeated: "Nelson."

He scrolled. "Got it. Nelson. She saved him under his first name?"

"How do we know she's not lying again?"

"Easy," Semyon said. "If it's not him, I tear off boyfriend's head. In front of her."

The phone beeped twice. Then died.

Vronsky closed his eyes.

CHAPTER 18

Zach's face throbbed like meat worked over with a mallet. Swelling pulled his skin tight, a constant, pulsing ache. He couldn't forget the look Keera gave him when he had to choose—shoot or surrender. And the tears. Her first tears. Had she seen his death? It felt close enough.

He has to explain this, Longhair had said. But explain what? They couldn't know Keera was psychic. That secret was the only edge they had.

They drove empty roads. No traffic. No pedestrians. Occasional driveways hinted at houses hidden in the dark. They passed through Sedona's deserted main street and began the long climb toward Flagstaff.

"In all my time," Longhair said, lighting a cigarette, "I have never had such a situation." He exhaled toward the driver, the A/C whisking the smoke away. He turned to Zach. "Who do you work for?"

"The *Chicago Post*."

"Bullshit, as you Americans say."

"I'm a journalist."

"Please. Do not insult me. My colleagues will tell you I have patience. Long after they lose theirs, I remain calm. This is my strength. But now, after today, I'm running on fumes. Understand?"

"Yes."

"Good. Here's how it works. Every time you lie, my large friend bounces your girlfriend's head off her shoulders. Understood?"

"Yes."

Zach couldn't shake the image—Keera doubling over from a blow. Her shoulders, up front, stiffened slightly. He didn't know what was worse: taking the hit himself or watching her take it.

"But how will you send another video if she's unconscious?" he asked.

"We already have a video," Longhair said. "Or we can work on less visible parts of her. No worries there."

Fucking animals.

He needed a new plan, and fast. They couldn't communicate. Couldn't move freely. He needed magic. Keera's kind.

"Anyone you target is going to want proof she's still alive and well," Zach said.

Longhair stared. "Will they ask for another glass? Why the glass?"

"I needed proof. I thought of a glass—common, domestic. What's the problem? Were you out of glassware, drinking from the bottle?"

Baldy rammed an elbow into Zach's ribs. "Keep respectful attitude."

Zach gasped and waited for the pain to settle. "It was a fair question," he said. "No need for unwanted physical contact."

Longhair studied him. "Possibly a coincidence. Let's go back. We first see you in Chicago. You visit your girlfriend, leave again. Nothing unusual. Typical boyfriend. Flashy car, nice clothes. Separate apartments to avoid commitment."

"It was mutual. We liked our space."

"You arrived most nights at eight, left near midnight. But after she disappears, you're not typical. You find her. No one does that without help. So—what help?"

The question he dreaded. Would the truth work?

"When Keera disappeared," he said, "I visited a psychic."

He dropped his right elbow defensively. Longhair speared an elbow into his other side.

Up front, Keera twitched.

"I tried the police. Hospitals. Got nowhere. There was nothing left but waiting. I couldn't."

"What did psychic say? 'Go to the apartment, get your girl'?"

He couldn't tell the full story. He barely believed it himself. Stick to the verifiable.

"She told me to go to a liquor store on 55th."

"And?"

"The clerk said two Russians came in every morning, bought Stolichnaya. Not the same two each time, but no more than three in rotation." Zach turned to Longhair. "He described all of you. Even mentioned the gray at your temples. Gave you an air of authority."

Let them think he had backing. Something bigger.

"What else?"

"Said the Russians might've walked from an apartment complex nearby. So I waited. You know the rest."

The driver muttered something in Russian. Longhair snapped back. The driver quieted.

They hit a major road and turned left.

"How did you guess Sedona?" Longhair asked.

Maybe he was buying it—or part of it.

"No psychic this time," Zach said. "I made a few calls. When I woke up—thanks for the knockout drops—the motel manager told me you'd left. I didn't know where. I thought airports first."

"You're so important airports give you passenger lists?" Longhair scoffed. "You must be government."

"I'm not. The manager gave me your plate. I called a friend at Homeland Security."

"I knew it," Longhair said. "I knew you were government."

"I'm not. I asked him to trace your plate. Feds have surveillance you can't imagine. You can't scratch your ass without a satellite watching."

"I know, I know. What happened to democracy? Freedom of speech?"

"It's vanishing. I wrote a long piece about it once."

"Forget it. I hate political articles. What happened after you rang your friend? Does he need cash? We want friends like yours."

"No chance. He spits on Russians."

Baldy grunted, but didn't jab him again.

"What did you do after the call?"

"He said your car had been tracked to an airfield. Occupants flew to Sedona."

"Which airport?" the driver asked, trying to trip him.

"He didn't say. Just what I needed to know."

"How did he know Sedona?"

"Every plane files a flight plan. Deviate, and you might get shot down."

Let them chew on that. Most of it was true. Let them waste time separating fact from fiction.

"You are such a good liar," Longhair said. "But you can't explain how you ended up in our car."

"That's the miracle. I saw two of you go into the store, car wasn't locked. Didn't know how long the shopping would take. I climbed into the back."

Another burst of irritation from the front, this time collecting a snarling response from Baldy. The two Russians had to be blaming each other for the door locks. A sharp word from Longhair and the bitching pair fell silent.

They turned off onto I-17 toward Flagstaff, then followed the road posted as Historic Route 66. Motels sprouted on every block. The driver chose one without comment.

Longhair said. "You check in. I'll follow. Write BVB 132 for plate. If I sense anything wrong, I kill you and the clerk. Then we find a safe place and play with your girlfriend."

There was no doubt he meant it. Now was not the time to try anything.

Longhair eased out of the SUV and beckoned Zach to follow.

The reception desk was manned by a short woman who found customers annoying, and talk expensive. She was skinny, with bleached hair tied up loosely, and a face crumpled as an autumn leaf.

Zach completed and signed the forms she shoved his way and slid them back.

"We have complimentary continental breakfast." She handed him keys and pointed to a small dining area off to one side.

"The room password is 'Wi-Fi'."

They parked outside a suite. The Russians ushered them inside. Longhair checked the windows and bathroom, opened every drawer and closet, dumped the hangers, iron, and board in the hallway.

"Empty pockets," he said.

Zach dropped a few bills on the bed. "You took everything last time. I grabbed some bucks from a friend."

"Very generous. You're paying for breakfast." Longhair pocketed the money.

"You get five minutes to refresh," he said. "Then we tie you to the bed."

He paused.

"Don't do sexing. My big friend will sense it. Then he'll join in. Previous clients found that uncomfortable."

CHAPTER 19

They held each other tightly, no words required. Keera grasped Zach's exhaustion, his despondency, stroked his back. She'd willed him to her, and he'd been caught and beaten. She'd directed him to Sedona and walked him into another beating. Her anguish compounded because she couldn't make things right.

"Let me see your face," she said, and clucked her tongue as she examined it. "Come in the bathroom, let me clean you up."

She dampened a cloth and gently wiped away blood streaks as he sat on the toilet seat. "There's a couple of cuts but the blood's clotted."

"I'll live a while longer then."

"A good deal longer. We'll have a plan worked out in a minute."

"I love your optimism, but they hold the aces and the guns. I'm sorry I messed up before, and now I've done it again."

"You didn't," she said quickly. "You got my message, and you found me, and that's a huge thing. How did you get to the motel?"

"What I told them was true, more or less. I met up with a psychic; she gave me the motel's whereabouts. The liquor store guy filled me in about the Russians."

"You saw a psychic?"

"Yeah." He grinned a little. "A bit out of character, what?"

"Desperate times, desperate measures, et cetera," Keera said, wanting to hug him to pieces but knowing he was too fragile for it. "How did you find the house?"

"Like I told them. Found a gun in the car but couldn't use it. It'd be a comedy of errors if it weren't so stupid."

His aura was muddy, with faint edges. His energy leaking out of him and she had too little hers to share.

"They'll buy another charger for my phone in the morning. We need to act before then."

"Why did they bring you here?" he asked. "Wait. Why did they grab you in the first place? I can't get my head around this. I've never heard of anyone's girlfriend being kidnapped before. But it happened to you."

"It's not about me," she said. "You saw the text message. It was to pressure my father into signing off on a contract with a certain Mr. Flint. This is all his doing." She spread her hands as if to indicate the parameters of their predicament.

"How's your head?" he asked. "That bastard can pack a punch."

"It stopped ringing after an hour." She smiled to let him know she was fine with it.

"No nausea, no confusion?"

"No concussion, Zach. I'm good."

"This is insane." He ruffled his hair like it would make it easier to think. "Flint? Who's Flint?"

"The person behind it all. My father to be shown his daughter captive and expected to acquiesce, hand over the contract to Flint. I guess the deal was worth many millions. It's all gone wrong now."

"That's why they brought you here?"

"Your previous appearance threw them. They contacted Flint, and he ordered them to come here."

"But they were moving you again when they found me."

"Because they killed Flint and his driver."

Zach blinked as he took this in. "Jesus. You saw this?"

"I heard two gunshots. After that Flint, now a floaty spirit, appeared in my room. He explained the falling out, and that the Russians would still try to extract money from my father."

He regarded her in disbelief. "The dead guy turned up and chatted with you?"

"Sure did. He's not going anywhere soon, wants revenge. If we can figure something out, he'll help us, too."

"I couldn't get dreams as confusing as this." He looked around the bathroom. "Is it me, or has it gotten colder in here?"

"Y'all together again. How sweet," Flint said. Standing by the door.

"What are you looking at?" Zach asked her.

"Mr. Flint," Keera said. "The nice person who organized our kidnapping. Guess he's back to talk."

"'Nice person?' I like that," Flint said.

"Did you miss school the day they taught uses of irony?" Keera asked.

"Right," Zach said. "I'll leave you two to chat, shall I?" He stood at the basin and examined his face.

"Were you in the car? I didn't see you," Keera asked Flint. He was fully intact now, but floating a foot off the floor.

A sheepish smile. "Above it. I get claustrophobic in crowded vehicles."

"How are your powers developing? Any more glass tricks? Have you moved on to shifting tables and rapping noises?"

"You're making fun of me, I know, but you need me to get y'all out of here."

"I need something. Not sure it's you."

"The way you talk to me? Makes the journey to the light a lot more attractive. I feel a pull toward it all the time now. Why should I hang around here, I ask myself."

"Sorry. It's just been a tough day," she said. "We have to escape those animals. Can you help, can you tell me what those goons are planning?"

"They're simple people with street cunning. They have only one idea: ask your father for money."

"Oh, the same as yours."

"Sister, my plan was fine. With you under control, I would have got the contract. Who knew you were psychic? Shit." He shook his head in disbelief at his unlucky break.

Her earlier anger with him reboiled. Keera slammed her hand against the shower screen causing Zach to look over, startled. She ignored him. Plenty of time to relate this silent conversation later.

"Haven't you learned any morals on the other side?" she barked at Flint. "You seem proud of your plan, even though it caused your death, and might cause ours."

"Old habits die hard." This with a smirk.

God, she wanted to strike him. "And, without you, how is

your corporation doing? Bet you've stepped back and taken a critical look at it too."

Flint grinned again. "You know what? I was leveraged up to my eyebrows. The last credit crunch removed all my sources of cheap money. Couldn't even get expensive money. The outfit wasn't mine anymore, hadn't been for a long time. It was an illusion. The banks own it, even if they don't know it for a few more weeks."

"Hasn't somebody noticed you're missing yet?"

"My personal assistant will get antsy if I don't make contact by tomorrow morning. Otherwise, nobody's looking for me. I can see where you're going with this. You want the police searching for my body and my car."

"It would help. Is the car outside one of yours?"

"A rental. Not in my name, or any company I'm associated with."

"Who owned the house you died in?"

"The place they shot me down like an animal, you mean? It's mine ... was mine. I stayed in it only a few times a year."

"Do you have family who expect you home soon?"

He cocked this head. "For a psychic, you sure ask a lot of questions. Aren't you supposed to know all this?"

"Psychics know nothing about a person until they're given that information by others. Do you have a family?" she repeated.

"Nope."

"Anybody care for you at all?" It wasn't a fair question to ask the recently deceased, but any goodwill she felt for him had evaporated long ago.

"Okay, I 'fess up; I was business-focused. Lost two wives, figured a third would be too expensive. No kids. What was the point? I was traveling all the time." He sounded regretful.

"I didn't ask you to justify your life," she said. "I'm trying to discover if there's a chance the police will be involved sooner rather than later."

"What's he saying?" Zach asked, looking around. "Is he going to be of any use?"

"Damn," Flint said. "He's just like you. Unfriendly, right from the get-go."

"He's had a hard day, too," she said. "Be nice, make allowances."

Flint glowered at her. "You two don't know what a hard day is. Neither of you got shot dead, for a start. You didn't have to find your feet in a brand-new world, and then discover you couldn't influence a single person anymore."

"You'll make it. You're the type who makes it anywhere."

"What's he saying?" Zach asked. "Are we working on a plan yet?"

"Our friend, Mr. Flint, is feeling sorry for himself," she said. "Instead, he should be apologetic that he landed us in this position."

"I am, a little," Flint said. "You don't make it easy, though. I'm surprised I even feel hurt by your attitude. I didn't expect to have feelings after I died."

"You've got everything you had before except a body. And in this case, that absence is an asset."

"That's the big question, isn't it? How do I use this asset?"

"Figure it out. You weren't stupid before, you're not stupid now. Keep an eye on next door, okay? In the meantime, we'd like some privacy."

Flint compressed his lips and vanished. Keera stalked from

the bathroom and sat on the bed.

"What was that all about?" Zach said as he followed her. "Isn't he helping us?"

"Not enough."

"What can he do, being dead and all that?"

"If I knew, I'd tell him. But he's a neophyte in his world. He can't operate easily so soon. At the moment he's good for unsettling them, but that's all."

"Yeah, I wanted to ask. How did he do that? Unsettle them."

"He moved a glass."

A quick laugh rippled through Zach. "That's why that long-haired guy asked me about it. He must think there's a link between me asking and the glass moving."

"It threw them, that's for sure. But Flint moved the glass before you mentioned it. Twice. I was there for the second time, and your request freaked them out. They can't get their minds around it."

"*I* can't get my mind around it. A glass just came to me when I needed proof you were still alive."

"Maybe you're getting a tiny bit psychic," she said, taking his hand and pulling him down to sit beside her. The usual electricity between them muted, both of them running on empty.

"It was a freakish guess. Let's not jump to conclusions, okay?"

She filled him in on what else she knew. "The long-hair'd one is Vronsky, the brute is Semyon, the fussy blond one is Yuri."

"How did you find all this out?"

"Soon as I could, I watched them. They're an unstable group, I can tell you that much."

"They're damn quick with the hands and elbows." Zach ran delicate fingers over his ribs.

"And guns." They linked arms and sat in silence. His presence had made their position more precarious. Now, the Russians could make credible threats to harm either of them if she or Zach refused to cooperate. They had maybe two hours to think up an escape plan. The first step was to gather more information.

"I have to sleep, recharge," she said, lying back on top of the covers. Zach nestled against her. "Don't," she said, wishing she didn't have to say it. "I'm going to travel."

He released her abruptly and rolled over. "Have a nice trip."

CHAPTER 20

Keera waited for Zach to fall asleep. When his breathing slowed into a shallow, even rhythm, she began the steps to relax her own body.

Minutes later, she slipped free. Hovered briefly in the room. No sign of Flint—a relief. But Bardo was absent, too, and that was less welcome. He'd be useful now. He'll come if I need him, she told herself. Hold that thought. Nail it to your heart.

She let herself drop into the rushing blackness and willed her spirit toward her father.

Nelson Miles sat at one side of a table in a boardroom somewhere, flanked by two aides. Three Russian businessmen faced him. At fifty, her father carried more grey than he liked, but he refused to dye it. As always, he wore a Savile Row suit, dark and exact, paired with a navy tie—a uniform meant to project control, reason, and a distaste for theatrics.

His mind sliced through negotiations like a surgeon with a thousand scalpels. Every version of the deal profitable.

An interpreter sat at the end of the table. Paperwork cluttered the surface—contracts, letters, printed emails. Behind them, the onion domes of the Kremlin gleamed beyond a wide window.

She drifted closer.

The Russians wanted more money—personally, not just for their companies. With the profits from oil, control of the process meant immense returns for the controllers. Her father was whittling away their demands with methodical precision. He'd give them enough to keep the deal alive, but not a drop more. They'd walk away thinking they'd won.

Until next time.

And if the kidnappers contacted him?

He'd react the same way. Negotiate. Trim the ransom. Delay. Squeeze leverage from the situation.

But Vronsky and his crew weren't built for drawn-out talks. They didn't have a safe base of operations or a contingency plan.

She saw it clearly now: once no quick payoff came, the hostages would be expendable.

She whirled back to the motel.

The Russians were gathered around the TV, watching an infomercial for a miracle cleaning spray. The room was dim. Yuri perched alert, lips pursed. Semyon lounged, brooding, barely watching but glancing often at Yuri. Still no Flint. Maybe he was off practicing ghostly glass tricks.

Vronsky muttered, "The boyfriend is lying. Crazy lies. But why?"

"You think he's government?" Yuri asked.

"He tracked her down twice. That takes resources. But then he locks himself in our car?" Vronsky shook his head. "And nobody came to rescue him. If he has backup, why let him stay trapped? They had time. They could've picked us off when we stepped outside—three shots, three corpses. Clean."

Keera realized she understood their Russian perfectly now. Better than before. That had to be Bardo's doing.

"It's a puzzle," Vronsky muttered, then turned to Semyon. "What do you think?"

"You asking me?" Semyon kept his eyes on the screen. "Ask the one who didn't check the trunk—after he knew it was unlocked."

"Who didn't lock the car in the first place?" Yuri snapped.

"Who's talking now—the forgetful one, or the careless one?"

"The one you tried to get the boyfriend to shoot."

"I was helping," Yuri said brightly. "Better than a shootout. If it came to that, some of us would be dead. You first. Be grateful."

"You meant it."

"Come on, Semyon," Vronsky said, warning in his voice. "We stand together or fall. Yuri used a tactic. That's all. He succeeded. Let it go."

Vronsky's nerves showed. He was worried Yuri would push Semyon too far.

"You're a wonderful guy," Yuri said with a grin. "It's an honor working with you."

Semyon ignored him.

"No more jokes," Vronsky said sharply. "He doesn't like it. And we've got bigger problems. The job's delayed, and soon people will notice she's missing."

"When?"

"She's an academic. Probably when she misses her first lecture with no excuse."

"That's Monday, maybe."

"Do we have notes on her movements before Monday?"

"No."

"Why not?"

"Because we only started surveillance on Tuesday."

"I told the American we needed earlier coverage," Vronsky muttered. "But he was on a budget. Idiot."

"The boyfriend's got the same issue," Yuri said. "Time. If he's telling the truth, his job's waiting too."

"If." Semyon scoffed. "He's no journalist. Somebody sent him to get the girl—quietly. That's why he laid down the gun."

"He was outgunned," Yuri countered. "He valued the girl more than his life."

"Give me two minutes alone with him," Semyon said. "Let's see if he can watch while his girl gets some Semyon action."

"You get something when you torture people," Vronsky said. "Not always the truth."

"And it's messy," Yuri added.

Semyon sneered. "You clean it up, I'll do the fixing. Hell, I'll even remind you."

"Forget it," Vronsky said. "We don't need answers we can't use. We've got tomorrow. Maybe part of Monday. If no one comes looking, we take them into the desert and end it."

"But we have fun first?" Semyon asked.

"If you want," Vronsky replied, weariness in his voice. "If you want."

He's giving up already, Keera realized.

The group was fracturing. Yuri was goading Semyon on purpose—and Vronsky was losing control. If no fast money came, everything would collapse. Panic surged in her chest. She fought it back. Panic clouded thought. She needed clarity. Needed answers.

The familiar tug came—an unseen hook yanking her from the room, through blackness, to a waiting figure.

Bardo.

"At last," she burst out. "I thought you'd left me. I called. I needed you." Emotion welled up, unconfined. "Where were you? Where the fuck were you?"

Bardo regarded her without blinking. "Finished venting?"

Her anger deflated like a balloon. Shouting at Bardo was like yelling at a pillow. Nothing bounced back.

"You're not looking your best," he said. "You've let yourself go the past couple days."

"What?" Her voice cracked. "You want me to pretty up? Give that ape one more reason to come at me?" Where was he going with this?

"Just an observation," he said. "Not all your assets are invisible."

A fleeting smile—and he was gone.

What was that supposed to mean? Get ready to die, leave a good-looking corpse?

CHAPTER 21

Kwitch. Zach didn't stir; a slight rattling as he breathed told her he was still deep in sleep. That gave her time before she broke the news: the kidnapping was almost over, a death sentence next.

That was the logic; her senses brought nothing up to contradict this. Only a few hours left to prepare for a situation that would crumble and collapse, with violence the only outcome.

The cryptic message from Bardo, about looking good? Made no sense. But she hoped it would, soon. Flint was too new in his world to be useful. Could Zach figure out an angle? Not quickly enough; battered and bewildered, his energy levels would take days to recharge. Even for a live wire like him.

Under the door, light flared, followed by loud surprised voices. Footsteps approached, and the door opened. She gazed steadily at Yuri's face; he stared back for a few seconds before withdrawing. He returned with ties and joined her and Zach by the wrist.

Zach awake now but unprotesting. Yuri pulled a dog chain

out of his back pocket and looped it from their wrists to the corner bed leg. He switched the overhead lights off, left them alone.

What had startled them?

"It was me," Flint said, materializing beside her. "I did it."

"Did what?" she asked aloud.

"What did what?" Zach asked.

"Flint's here."

"Messed with the lights," Flint said. "That's what. They freaked out. I flicked the television off too, and then back on, and changed the channel. Can you believe they watch The Shopping Network?"

"What did they say?"

"First, they thought it was a fault in the TV. Then Yuri said it was you messing with them. He thinks you might have something going. He's kinda clued in about this stuff, you know. Watch him."

"I watch all of them."

"He's got a taste for killing now. His gun compensates for his lack of clout in this group."

"Yuri shot you? Not Semyon?" This was news.

Zach lifted his head.

"Correct," Flint said.

"I thought Semyon was the enforcer."

"Yuri got trigger happy, he still itchin' to go again."

Shit. "What does Vronsky think?"

"He's about to call the whole deal off; got government surveillance on his mind, and that makes him jittery. He's not letting on, though. Semyon only wants to eat, fuck, and shoot people; especially wants to fuck and shoot you."

"You keep saying that. I wish you wouldn't," she said. "I can't operate if I get too nervous."

"What's he saying?" Zach asked, looking at her and around the room.

"I'll tell you in a minute," she said.

Flint took a breath, although he didn't need one, didn't need any. "I know you won't believe me, but I feel bad about you. There I was thinking numbers and angles and moves, and not a single thought about you. I apologize."

"While apologies are in order, I'll say sorry for being ungracious to you when you tried to help earlier."

"I accept your apology."

"But it was because I was so angry you were the one responsible."

"If you qualify an apology, it doesn't sound so good."

"Okay. You're right. I was explaining, that's all."

"Don't explain. Just say sorry."

"Sorry." She couldn't believe it. This guy was dead, and he was still browbeating her.

"Let's move on," Flint said. "I got a plan. I can mess with their phones and turn all the lights off."

"You think Zach and I should sneak out in the dark? Like that's going to happen. There'll be enough light from outside for them to see us coming out of this room. Also, we're a little tied up here."

"No, of course not. But if nothing works for them soon, they'll move you and try again elsewhere."

"How is that a plus?"

"Every time they have to move, they risk being seen with you two. Or being remembered. Or you might attract help while they're busy moving."

She considered these possibilities. "They'll shoot us if we try anything. They threatened that, and I believe them. Others might die."

"Okay, let's keep it simple," he said. "If I stop them from using your phone, they'll be stymied, won't they?"

"How?"

"If your phone doesn't work, they can't call your pa— they have no number to call. It's on your dead phone. Can't be retrieved. You can't recall it, no matter how much they threaten you, because that number was in the phone contacts list. You never memorized it, you didn't need to memorize it."

"That still sounds dangerous to me. If their plan is dead, so are we."

"You got a better plan?" Flint looked at Zach lying next to her. "What about him? Is he an asset or just your handbag?"

Anger propelled her upright. "Get out," she spat. He gave her a startled look but disappeared.

Zach rolled against her. "You sounded mad at him."

"Nothing, he gets me so annoyed." It was bad enough she found it hard to control her own temper. They didn't need both of them snapping at Flint, a possible savior. "He's got a plan. Half of one, anyway. In the meantime, he's watching them."

"Even half a plan is good. What's he thinking?"

"He's had success manipulating electricity. He thinks he can shut down my phone. Then they can't call my father."

"So then they give up, shoot us and leave."

"That's what I said." So we have to act while they're figuring out why the phone won't work."

Zach sat up, arched his back, rotated his shoulders. "Semyon's the tough nut out there. I can thump the other two hard enough for them to stay down. If I get the chance. Look what happened when I tried to jump them last time. I had a gun and surprise working for me, and I still lost out."

"It was worth trying, Zach. At least they're bewildered and unsure of things."

"Exactly. We should confuse them even more."

"Are you kidding? They are so jumpy now, anything new might make them react badly. Anyway, how are we going to do this?"

Zach faced her. "We use what we've got."

"Which is?"

"You."

Keera tilted her head. "I don't have mysterious physical powers, Zach. I only know stuff others don't."

"Exactly. And it's amazing stuff. Stuff that could shock them."

He could hardly keep still, like a great idea was bouncing around inside him, demanding to be announced.

"What if you chat to their loved ones who've passed on," he said. "You might get a whole heap of information. Think about it. You'll get details of their lives, crucial stuff we can use."

"We'll get details, all right. Humdrum stuff. Like Yuri should eat more vegetables, Vronsky shouldn't neglect his family. You've never chatted to the dead, Zach. Their interests can be quite personal and mundane."

"I don't know until I see what material turns up. They strongly suspect a secret agency behind us. If we give them pieces of information we couldn't normally know, it'll confirm their suspicions."

There was a fresh sparkle in his eyes that she hated to stamp out. "It sure will. They yank out their guns and empty them on us."

"They'll do that anyway if we don't act."

He had an irrefutable point. She knew it better than he did. She could wait for Bardo to come up with suggestions; she could wait for Flint to create opportunities to escape, or she could wait for both of them to die. The waiting was almost worse than death. "So how do we work this?"

"You chat to the dead zone—"

"Please, Zach, I hate that jargon."

"Okay. You call up a bunch of dead relatives and—"

"I can't call up anybody. I can only ask."

"Right. You ask. You talk to them who turn up and tell me what they say. I write it down. Scrub that, I can't leave notes. I'll remember it all."

"Those on the other side can get quite voluble. You sure you can get it all?"

"You forget what I do for a living? I'm used to taking in information. I have terrific recall. And if we have gaps, it won't matter. The Russians won't question me too closely. They'll have secrets from each other. And they'll be nervous I might blow one of their personal secrets before they can stop me."

"What will you say when they ask why you didn't mention it before?"

He gave a confident grin she knew was all bravado. "Easy. I say I tried to rescue you without exposing information we have, but it didn't work. I'll explain they've fallen into a bigger operation than they know. To prove it, I'll tell them whatever you found out.

"And we'll walk out the door waving goodbye?"

"Once they believe we're not alone, the whole situation

changes for them. I don't know how it'll pan out, of course, but I'll play it as it unfolds. By the time we're finished they'll be non-plussed big time". He rolled the word around in his mouth again. "Nonplussed. They'll be open to our suggestions.

"Like what?"

"They let us walk, and they get to go home. No police, no charges."

She stared off into space. It was a thin plan, not even a plan, a hope. But if she got good information, it could work. "It doesn't feel right. Using the dead to fool the living."

"You have rules about that?"

"Not that I've heard of. If they don't approve, they don't have to cooperate."

"We have to try; there's nothing else we have."

She sat up straighter, swung her legs over the side of the bed.

"You're right. We have to do this." She drew deep breaths. "The last time I tried this a couple of years ago, I got a heap of pushy relatives coming through, all trying to talk at once. I bet there's a whole bunch out there waiting for me to open up."

"That's terrific news. Because one of them will help us escape this madness."

CHAPTER 22

Keera sat still on the bed, calming her body, working through her meditations, her chakras, opening her channels to the next world. Points of lights appeared like stars coming into view after sundown. The closest light materialized into an older woman. Only a partial. A handsome head, hair pulled back in a bun. Behind her, other points grew brighter, other spirits picking up that a channel was open.

"I am aunt of Yuri," the woman said, eager to talk, her words a burst of heavily accented English.

"I've got an aunt. Yuri's a nice boy, she says," Keera related to Zach. "He got mixed up at an early age with the wrong people."

"Where does he live now?"

"Moskva, Leninsky Prospekt." Then Keera's voice changed, picked up the aunt's inflections. "He is good boy, he cleans his home. He goes to IKEA for best furniture."

"What's her name?" Zach asked.

"Agata. I am sister of Yuri's father. He, too, is with me."

Keera passed this on.

Zach pushed for more. "Has he any other close relatives that are still alive?"

"Yuri's mother is alive but close to death. She needs medicine for pain. Yuri promised to send her the latest drugs from America."

"Nice boy, thinking of his mom like that," Zach said. "What's wrong with her?"

Keera doubled over as a fiery claw gripped her. "Cancer," she gasped. "Liver cancer. God, that's awful." She straightened up as the pain subsided. An image of a woman lying in an open casket came to her. "She hasn't got long. Yuri won't see her again."

Another figure pushed to the front. "His father's here," she announced.

The father cleared his throat as if to start a long speech. "I am sorry for Yuri that I was drunk so often. Tell him not to drink, and to stay away from such bad companions. He can achieve what he wants if he does this. He has much talent."

"He says tell Yuri to leave the bottle alone," she told Zach.

"Okay, but can we get the name of Yuri's bank?"

"Globexbank," the Russian told her, and she passed it on to Zach.

"And the father's name?" Zach asked.

The Russian drew himself up. "Vladimir Konstantinovich Buteyko."

"Impressive-sounding name," Zach said, repeating it aloud when she passed it on. "We have enough about Yuri. He's not the main problem here. The other two? Any of their loved ones turned up yet? Hard to believe Semyon's got anyone who loves him."

She waited for several minutes. More lights crowded into the room. Word had gotten out that a portal was open to the physical world. She told them silently to get in a line.

"What's happening?" Zach asked.

"Many people coming up. I'm trying to organize them."

A nervous young man, barely past his youth, waited to speak. She felt he was important and acknowledged him.

"My father is here," the man said. "He can't see me. I want to talk to him."

"Who is your father?" she asked.

"Andrei Sergeyovich Vronsky," the man replied stiffly. "I am his son, Sasha. I have passed to this life, just yesterday. He doesn't know."

"I got Vronsky's son. Name is Sasha. He passed over yesterday and wants to tell his father."

Zach jerked upright. "You're kidding. This is big news. Fucking huge. Vronsky's son is dead, we know it and he doesn't. This'll rock him back on his boot heels. How'd he die?"

"It was Tajik heroin," Sasha replied. "Where is this place? I see my father in next room but he doesn't answer me." Confused, he kept looking around the room as if searching for some clue. He faded from view. More lights pushed forward, clamoring to be heard. She ignored them.

"He's gone," she said.

"This guy's gold. If I can tell Vronsky his son died, and he can verify it, we're home. Rock-solid credibility."

"Do we have enough information yet?"

"We need their full names. That'll rock them. As far as they're concerned, we don't know any of them. They never introduced themselves, did they?"

"Yuri's last name is Buteyko. I overheard them use it before, and now we have confirmation from his father. And Sasha gave me Vronsky's. I'll try for Semyon's." She asked the gathered lights if any of them wanted to leave a message for Semyon. No one materialized, no one spoke to her.

"I'm getting nothing for him," she told Zach. "He seems unloved on the spirit side."

"Who'd have thought it?" Zach said. "A lovely guy like that. Nature's gentlemen."

The lights had lost patience, talked at once, voices rising, urgent, some frantic. She picked up Yuri's name several times. "All I'm getting is more of Yuri's folks. He's the darling of the family, and they're disappointed the way he's turned out."

"Disappointed? He's a kidnapper, for a start. That's a life sentence, isn't it? Also a murderer. He'll be behind bars so long, we'll have colonized the moon by the time he gets out."

"I'm not debating with them, Zach, I'm passing on their hopes."

The voices grew stronger, cramming into her head and trampling her thoughts. "I have to stop; such a headache from their chatter." She drained her glass and stared at the floor. The lights faded and disappeared.

Zach mulled over his information, mentally sorting it into bullet points. He had Vronsky's name and his son's. That alone was a grenade in the room. He could inform Vronsky that his son was dead—devastating news. If Vronsky could confirm it. He could tell Yuri they knew of his background, even knew his bank.

"The relatives, they were more helpful than you expected."

"We got lucky," Keera said. "Yuri's kin disapproved of his life and wanted him to change. Sasha was newly dead and confused. He didn't quite grasp what we were doing. I wouldn't rely on his support if he comes back." She sipped at the glass before realizing it was empty. "Don't we need more information than that?"

"Not really. Suggestion and innuendo go a long way mixed with smatterings of facts. That's how celebrity media works, you may have noticed."

If pressed for more, he'd say he hadn't read the complete files. The information he had was going to do their heads in—that much was obvious. What then? Would they kill and run? How could he cut a deal?

He recalled interviewing experienced politicians and government officials. People adept at stonewalling but revealing enough facts to keep you interested. That's the way he had to run it. Knowledgeable, but not interested in bargaining. Make them see that their best interests lay in doing what he suggested. Either it worked or they were dead. Him first, then Keera after suffering God knows what. He wiped a hand over his face, found he was clenching his teeth.

She hadn't mentioned Bardo. What was happening there? Wasn't he the guy who helped with suggestions and tips? What was the point of having a guide if you had to do all the work yourself?

Keera reached over and put her empty glass on the bedside table. As soon as she let go, it slid across the table.

Zach said, "Hey, Flint, you're supposed to be spooking the goons next door, not me."

"What's he—?" She turned around, glared at the space in front of Zach. "This is not the time to play games."

She listened a moment, then said, "I'll tell him when you're around, you don't need to do stunts like that." A moment more, then she stiffened, almost imperceptibly.

"What's he saying?" Zach asked her.

She didn't meet his eyes. "He says the glass moving is a sign to you he's with you. And he'll be wanting to help."

"Nice of him." She was holding something back.

She listened to thin air again. "He's got Vronsky's bank numbers and the account password."

Zach blinked a couple of times as he absorbed this. "Jesus, the password? How did he manage that?"

"He says Vronsky checked his bank account on his phone app. He watched when he pulled up the details. Got the lot."

"Sounds like Flint could have an amazing career as a bank robber. If he had any use for the money."

"Death is full of ironies, don't you think?"

"More then I expected. So now, if Vronsky gets the ransom, we know how to get it back."

She gazed at him with disbelief. "You think we'll live long enough after any ransom's paid to be interested in money?"

"It helps to be confident. Get the details off him, I'll find a way to use them."

"I'm sure you will," she said. "I'm sure you will."

CHAPTER 23

Bobby Flint watched as the paramedics lifted his body from the car and laid it on a stretcher. His guard's corpse was already in the ambulance, covered with a sheet.

Deputies stood nearby, sweating in the morning sun, damp patches spreading across their uniforms. The scrubby desert brush offered no shade.

Flint scanned the scene, searching for his guard's afterlife presence. Wasn't a newly dead supposed to linger near their bodies? He had—at least, he hadn't gone far. But no wispy, see-through version of the man appeared.

A large man approached the stretcher, surveying the bodies with faint distaste. Flint recognized him—Sergeant Lovejoy. Big, but not jolly. Hadn't been quick to accept his hospitality, like it was a crime to get a free drink or something.

"We have any ID from the plates yet?" he asked a deputy.

A squad car radio crackled nearby. A deputy hustled over.

"It's Bobby Flint's car," he said. "The guy with the busted-up face might be him. Build matches."

Lovejoy walked to the stretcher, lifted the sheet. "That's him, I'm sure of it. Bobby usually checks in when he's in town. Didn't this time."

"Why'd he check in? Had a record or something?" The question came from a green deputy, Flint could tell—awkward posture, overly deferential.

"You don't know this, Sierra, but Bobby Flint was born here. Left early, made a pile in Texas, but always came back. Spent good money in the county. When he visited, he asked us to keep an eye out for strangers—said a rich man attracts trouble." He turned back to the stretcher. "Looks like he was right this time."

"Who's the other guy?" Sierra asked.

"Bobby always traveled with a guard. That'll be him. Entry wound's at the temple, a quick execution job."

"Should we check Flint's house?"

"First port of call." Lovejoy moved toward his cruiser. He walked fast for a big man—like a bear on a mission. "He had a concealed carry license here. You find a gun?"

"Nope," said another deputy. "Forensics found nothing."

Lovejoy shot a look at the crime scene techs. "When are you guys going to tell me something I don't already know?"

One of them shrugged. "Not many prints. Obvious surfaces wiped clean. GSR tests should tell us more by this afternoon."

The medical examiner looked up from his notes. "Time of death: somewhere around nine or ten last night."

"About eight hours before those kids spotted the car," Lovejoy said, then yanked open the driver's door and slid in.

Sierra hovered uncertainly, then climbed into the follow car with two other deputies.

"What'd I say?" Sierra muttered.

"It wasn't you, Romeo," said the driver. "Frank knew Bobby. Flint always invited the boys over when he was in town. Serious liquor cabinet. Bought him a lot of goodwill."

That's true, Flint thought. And now it's payback time.

Ten minutes later, Lovejoy and his team rolled into Flint's driveway.

"Place smells empty," Lovejoy said.

Smells empty? What kind of procedural manual was he using?

"Circle around, cover the exits," Lovejoy told one deputy. "You," he said to Sierra, "turn my car around, in case we have a chase situation."

"But there's no other car here, sir."

Lovejoy gave him the look. "Some people still use their feet."

Sierra sighed and got in the car. Lovejoy didn't wait. He moved up the drive with Deputy Cooper trailing behind.

Cooper, Flint thought. I remember him. Liked his booze, top shelf only.

Lovejoy drew his gun, stepped beside the front door, and knocked with his free hand.

"Police! Open the door."

No answer. He knocked again, then tried the knob. The door swung open. Cooper raised his weapon and followed. Flint drifted after them, back to the room where he'd died.

"Two bodies in the car, two blood pools here," Lovejoy said. "That's helpful." He nodded to the hall. "Open the back. Let your partner in. Then check upstairs." The deputies moved. Lovejoy gave the kitchen and bathrooms a once-over.

"The place is empty," Cooper reported after the sweep.

"Call the body boys. You two, check the perimeter."

The techs entered, gloved up, and got to work. The place was spotless. No food wrappers, no bottles. No useful prints.

The Russkies were thorough—when they remembered to be. Flint wandered into the kitchen. The dishwasher's red light blinked. A cycle had finished. He peeked inside. Spotless glasses, forks, knives. No prints there.

In the living room, techs were crouched under the coffee table and sofas. One withdrew a scrap of paper.

"A receipt, Sergeant," he said, sealing it in a plastic bag.

"From where?"

"Monty's."

"Sedona?"

"Yep. Sandwiches and vodkas."

"Vodka? Bobby was a JD guy."

"Must've been his guests."

"Does it list the cashier?"

"No, but it's time-stamped. We'll get the name from that."

"What time?"

"Nine-fifteen."

Lovejoy turned to Sierra. "Get a copy without touching the original. Then haul your ass to Monty's. Get a description of whoever bought that stuff. If the cashier's off shift, track him down. He's the key."

Unbelievable. Flint beamed. That stupid receipt jammed under the sofa might blow the whole thing. If they stay in their motel another couple hours, they're done.

A tech approached Lovejoy again.

"Five bedrooms. Only one used. Bed's barely rumpled—someone lay on top but didn't sleep in it."

"How many people?"

"Four small glasses in the dishwasher—possibly for drinking vodka. One larger glass too. Same style as the tumblers in the bathrooms. We figure it came from the one that's missing its tumbler."

"Which bathroom?"

"Upstairs. Room with the barely used bed. So maybe five people total."

"Flint, his bodyguard, and three others."

"Could be more. If the guard wasn't drinking, we're talking six."

Lovejoy nodded. "Let's say they were here at nine-thirty. Bobby and his guard die soon after. So the killers—what, eat first? Eat after?"

"After. Killings over, adrenaline drops, they get hungry."

"So maybe things went bad. Bobby could be abrasive."

Abrasive? I was assertive, Flint thought. Taking charge of a tricky situation.

Outside, Lovejoy squinted at the gravel.

"Well, we've driven all over it, so no wheel tracks now."

"Right," said a tech. "But this is crushed stone—and not local. If we find the missing car, it might have some stuck in the treads. That'd link it."

"Anything else?"

"No mixers. Just vodka."

Lovejoy frowned. "Who drinks vodka straight?"

"Russians. Poles. Ukrainians. Balts. East Europeans, basically."

Lovejoy rubbed his neck. "They stand out around here. As

soon as they open their mouths. Shouldn't be hard to find some-one who saw them."

He paused, eyes on the house.

"Bobby wasn't perfect," he muttered. "But he didn't deserve this."

Damn right I didn't, Flint thought.

CHAPTER 24

The door opened and Yuri walked in.

"We find interesting breakfast now. You want something? I can offer coffee with donuts or coffee with Danish."

Zach sat up and planted his feet on the floor. "Yo, Yuri. How's things? You going near a drugstore this morning? Don't forget your mother's medication. I hear she's suffering."

Yuri stopped. "What you say about my mother?" His tone stayed casual, but his face tightened.

"Just saying you should look after her. Otherwise, she might join your Aunt Agata before her time. I'll have coffee and donuts. My friend'll take the Danish. She prefers tea, not coffee."

Yuri glanced at Keera—still unmoving—then turned and left, closing the door behind him. Zach heard low murmurs outside, Vronsky's voice answering.

Semyon appeared, removed the door chain but kept their wrists bound, then pushed them out.

Yuri was pacing. Vronsky, settled in an armchair, gestured to the couch opposite. Zach and Keera sat.

"Why do you call him 'Yuri'?" Vronsky asked, nodding toward him.

"Because that's his name," Zach replied. Take it slow. Give them just enough.

"What do you know of his mother?"

"Just what I read in the files. Can't remember much. Didn't have time to study."

"It's not what you recall that matters," Vronsky said. "It's how you know anything at all."

"We know a lot about the people we need to."

"You said you were just boyfriend. Now you say different."

"It's complicated. Boyfriend-girlfriend, sure. But there's more."

"How much more?"

"That, Andrei Sergeyovich Vronsky, I'm not willing to say."

Vronsky froze. Yuri snapped something in Russian.

"So," Vronsky said, "if you know my name, you know it's very dangerous for you."

Zach smiled, hoping it looked confident. "If I know your name, Mr. Vronsky, be assured my organization does too. You've got nowhere to run, nowhere to drive, nowhere to fly."

Vronsky barked orders in Russian. Yuri snapped something in Russian. Vronsky ignored him, stayed on Zach.

"What do you want?"

"You crashed something we set up. We want you gone. You're jamming the works."

"You are government, yes?"

Zach shrugged. "Can't say."

"Then why didn't your people wipe us out?"

"Too messy. It's a delicate op. We hate publicity. It got tricky when you took my friend—worse when you killed Flint and his guard."

Came out easy. Keep him leaning forward, not stepping back.

Vronsky gave a smile full of teeth but empty of warmth. "You know shit."

"Vronsky, we know everything."

"Not possible."

"But true."

He didn't show much, but Zach could tell the impact had landed. Time to push while he was still off balance.

"Can I suggest something? I leave with my friend. You try your luck escaping the cops."

"Why would I let you go? Maybe nice girl is bait. I let her walk, American agents crash through door and shoot, shoot, shoot."

"We wouldn't do that."

"Of course. Such angels you work for."

"We're not interested in the murders. That's a police thing. We've got bigger problems. You want to leave first? Go ahead."

Vronsky's face changed. Not fear—calculation. Zach saw it: the weighing up of whether to kill two more witnesses.

Yuri spoke. "You might've overheard our names, but you don't know everything."

Zach ignored him, inspected his fingernails—grimy now. Then looked at Vronsky.

"Your son Sasha? You call him today?"

Vronsky's face didn't move. Just one blink.

"You missed your chance. He died yesterday. Overdose. Shipment was purer than he expected."

Vronsky didn't flinch. Just reached for his phone, dialed,

wiped his face. No answer. He hung up and made another call.

"*Gde Sasha?*" he snapped. Halting, uncertain words answered. He muttered something and ended the call, then stared at Zach with a new intensity.

"What do you want?"

Not denying it. Just adjusting.

"We leave. You go wherever."

"Don't be stupid. No guarantee."

"I can't give one. But Flint wasn't nobody. The locals will be looking hard. You've got less than a day before they close in."

Zach looked at Yuri. "Find any nice items here for your apartment on Leninsky Prospekt? IKEA's fine, but don't pretend you don't have taste. Just because you were once FSB…"

Yuri clamped his mouth shut. Vronsky barked more Russian. Yuri nodded and left the room.

Semyon didn't like it. He glowered, then glanced at Keera again. Grunted something. Vronsky grunted a sharp response. Zach figured Vronsky had made his decision. They were abandoning the site, and Semyon didn't want to lose Keera.

Yuri returned with his pack. Zipped it closed.

"You agree?" Zach asked. "You're leaving now?"

Vronsky didn't answer. Just stared through him.

Don't rush, Zach thought. As long as they're holding us, we've got value. Vronsky wouldn't trust a maybe-agent. And the news about Sasha? He'd taken it better than expected—on the outside.

"So, what's your plan? Stay here forever?"

"I am thinking she comes with us, you, maybe not."

"Nobody leaves this motel without our agreement."

"Who needs agreement when we have girl?"

"How far behind do you think the police are? Flint was a big name. You can bet the sheriff and his posse are working their butts off to find the killer." Sounded too eager. He had to dial it back.

"Posse? What is 'posse'?"

"His team. They're coming, Vronsky. Every minute you waste they're closer."

He used Vronsky's name again—reminding him how exposed he was.

"They come, they find you two dead."

"And they leave you three dead. They don't waste time."

He sounded like a B-movie spy. But it was all he had.

"You're saying we're under surveillance now?"

"You've been tracked since you took Keera. These aren't weather satellites either. They can read your credit card number when you pay for lunch."

"*O Boze moj*," Yuri muttered.

Vronsky turned on him with a guttural snarl—pain, rage, and disbelief in one savage sound. It shut Yuri up fast.

"You have no future," Zach said. "No chance to extort anything."

Keera stayed quiet, as if waiting for a perfect outcome only she could see. Zach wished he had her faith.

"How do you know about the money?" Vronsky asked. "Or that we won't get it?"

"Forget the money. I've got instructions to reach an agreement. After that, if we're not free, backup moves in."

Vronsky barked at Semyon, who stepped to the window and closed the curtains.

Zach pressed. "You planning to live here now? Is that the big play?"

"You give stupid choices. Leave and get shot. Stay and get arrested. Such good options."

"You have to trust me. We don't—"

"I trust nothing you say. You were boyfriend. Now agent. I believe both. You lie when useful."

He stood. "You know more than I expected. But no matter. We take girl. You stay. You explain to your people we want money. Then we release her."

"That won't work. Who would believe you?"

"We have to believe each other—or die. This is the way forward."

Zach tried to argue again, but Vronsky cut him off.

"Enough. This is how it will be."

He gave instructions. Yuri opened the door, tensed, and stepped outside toward the motel office. Vronsky and Semyon held still, waiting. No shots.

Zach looked at Keera. She placed a hand over his.

"I'll be fine," she whispered.

She was lying.

If she left with them, she vanished. No more clues. No trail. This was his third attempt to save her. Third failure.

He gripped her hand like it could change something.

Vronsky dragged the bags to the door. Semyon cleared bottles and glasses, wiped the latter clean, packed the rest.

Yuri returned, agitated. Grabbed his pack and spoke quickly.

"Police are fast, as you said," Vronsky told Zach. "Reception woman wouldn't look Yuri in the eye. Maybe someone called her. We go now."

He raised his gun and gestured at Keera.

"Let's go."

"No chance," Zach said, jumping up.

Semyon moved faster. His fist slammed into Zach's temple. He crashed over the sofa, arms and legs disconnected from his brain.

Keera crawled to him, pulled his head into her lap, whispered something—but he couldn't make it out. Pain and fog clouded everything.

Semyon yanked her away and dragged Zach to the sink. Tied him to the drainpipe. Zach had no strength left to resist.

Vronsky knelt in front of him.

"You say hello to police. If we don't kill you, maybe your people won't kill us. They don't care about you anyway. They didn't even give you a gun."

Semyon duct-taped Zach's mouth. Two strips.

Vronsky held up Zach's phone. "This I leave. You will talk to her father. Make sure the money is ready when we call."

He slid the phone across the floor, just out of reach.

"One more thing. If we see you again, we'll know you broke the deal. We kill you both. No question."

Semyon placed his gun against Keera's ribs, lifting her coat so it looked like he had an arm around her.

Yuri clicked the SUV unlocked. He got behind the wheel. Semyon and Keera followed. She resisted in the doorway, looked back.

Mouthed something. Zach couldn't catch it.

Vronsky gave her a shove. They vanished.

Doors slammed. Engine roared. The SUV disappeared.

Zach wiped his face against his shoulder. The pain was fading.

He tried again to recall what Keera had whispered.

Nothing. Memory flattened by the blow.

What had she mouthed at him? He visualized her at the door, her lips moving in exaggerated slowness, and this time, it came: Flint, she had said.

The dead guy who was supposed to be helping.

Watch for Flint, she'd meant.

"It's a good time to start, buddy," Zach thought. "The perfect time to start."

CHAPTER 25

Zach chewed at the tape but couldn't get a grip. He examined the pipe for weakness—nothing obvious. Wriggling into a semi-crouched position, his head level with the sink, he rubbed his face against the porcelain, trying to catch an edge.

Too smooth. The enamel gave him nothing.

He lifted his head to the mirror. A new face blinked back—split skin on the bruised side of his face, blood trickling through yesterday's swelling. Still taped, still stuck.

Nothing to do but wait for the maid. Early still—she wouldn't be around for a couple of hours.

The front door stood ajar, allowing a pencil-thin view of the outside world. A car cruised past. Another. Doors clicked open —but no slams. Maybe deputies. Or a SWAT team. He imagined high-powered rifles behind car doors, men flanking the entrance. Ready.

He tried to yell, but produced only a muffled grunt.

Shadows flitted past the gap. He lowered himself to the floor, made like a corpse.

Might save him from a hail of bullets.

Then came the megaphone. "This is the police. Come out with your hands in the air."

Great suggestion. Wish I could.

"You have one minute or we will open fire."

Another voice cut in—a woman.

"The hell you will!"

She wasn't shy.

"This is my place, and there'll be no shooting."

Voices answered, lowered now. She wasn't buying it.

"They've gone. I told you—they're gone. I saw them. There's nobody in there." More murmuring. Then: "Oh, for heaven's sake."

Footsteps—light, fast—ran to the door.

It flew open. The motel receptionist stood there, a loose strand of hair falling across her face. She blew it aside with a sharp puff.

"The fuck you doing to my sink?"

Deputies flooded in behind her—guns drawn, padded vests, wary eyes. One of them wore no uniform, no armor either; his size alone would have made either difficult to wear.

"He's gagged, sir," one deputy said.

"And tied," another added.

"Check the other rooms," barked the big man, and the two peeled off.

Zach heard crashes and thumps; he guessed doors were being kicked open. Grunts of disappointment followed. More uniforms and badges and caps crowded in.

The big man knelt easily and ripped off the duct tape. No gentle touch.

"I'm Detective Sergeant Lovejoy. Where's your pals?"

Zach lifted his wrists. Lovejoy sliced them free with a penknife.

"Where's your pals?" he repeated.

"They're not my pals. Been gone ten minutes. Black BMW SUV. Arizona plates starting ACN."

Lovejoy flipped to a page in his pad. "Wrong, young fella. Our information says otherwise."

"Where'd you get your number?"

"The one they gave when they checked in."

Zach gestured toward the woman, now straightening the coffee table and eyeballing deputies like they were overgrown children.

"They told her the wrong number. I saw the plates. She didn't check them, did she?"

Lovejoy looked at her. She shook her head.

"Cooper," he barked. A deputy stepped forward.

"Give this partial number to dispatch, too."

Lovejoy tore out the page and handed it over.

Zach got to his feet, planting them wide against the dizziness. "Do you know who you're chasing?"

"A bunch of killers."

"Three males. They're Russians. Also my girlfriend—they kidnapped her in Chicago yesterday. She's with them."

Lovejoy stiffened. "Kidnappers? Christ. Name?"

"Keera Miles."

"Description?"

"Twenty-five, long black hair, blue eyes. Denim jacket, print dress, ankle boots." It didn't begin to describe the Keera he knew.

Lovejoy scribbled, found Cooper again, and handed over another page. "Get this over the air, now. Three Russian males, holding a woman named Keera Miles. That's the description."

Zach turned to the basin. Lovejoy stopped him.

"Don't contaminate a crime scene. Medic will check your face outside."

A crime scene. It was more than a fucking crime scene. It was the end of his world as he knew it.

"Where to?" Yuri asked.

"A bigger city," Vronsky replied. "Vegas or Phoenix. Haven't decided."

The girl sat beside him in the back, unusually quiet. He preferred it that way today.

Sasha. Dead. Only a dozen hours ago. And somehow, they knew.

"Take your time," Semyon said. "We've got fifteen minutes before the cops close off the roads."

"Vegas is best. Full of tourists. We won't stand out. But it's farther—more road, more patrols."

Semyon nodded.

"Vegas. I like. Quality hookers."

"That's not a factor," Vronsky muttered.

"Small town, this one," Semyon said. "How many cops they got?"

"Enough. Plus sheriff's department."

"So, diversion. We torch the car. Or burn a store. Pull them off the roads."

"Think, Semyon. They're already circulating our plates. Highway Patrol, locals, hundreds of eyes."

"What's your plan if we're stopped?" Yuri asked.

"First, we get a new car. There's no reason to stop us if we are not three men and a girl and we can hide the girl."

Yuri turned at a sign. Unity Church of Flagstaff. "It's Saturday. Wedding day."

They pulled into the leafy lot. Dozens of cars scattered under the trees. Yuri backed into a space. "Which one's best?"

A maroon Cadillac pulled in. The driver was ancient, peering over the wheel like a suspicious prairie dog.

"That one," Yuri said. "Semyon, take the keys."

Semyon shot him a look. "Since when do you give orders?"

"It's obvious. You're the muscle. I'm the strategist."

"You're a prissy woman is what you are."

"Semyon," Vronsky cut in. "Handle the driver. Yuri, swap plates."

Yuri grabbed a screwdriver from the bag and headed off. He walked past several cars before selecting one and unscrewing the rear plate.

Semyon approached the Cadillac. The old man was already out, standing by the door, wary and still. Semyon extended his hand for the keys. The man hesitated, offered them.

The Russian's hand swallowed his. The other hand smashed into the man's chin.

No resistance. The old man crashed back against the car, then slid down, head lolling to his chest.

"No!" Keera cried.

"Shut up," Vronsky snapped, dragging her out of the car.

The old man didn't twitch. Blood tracked down his throat. Semyon was efficient—he'd give him that.

Semyon stuffed the body into the BMW's trunk. The girl

watched in siilence.

Yuri replaced the Cadillac's plate and shut the SUV's engine off. Locked it. Semyon was already behind the wheel of the Caddy.

"Since when are you the driver?" Yuri asked.

"Since I got bored watching you fuck up." He started the engine. "Get in or get left behind."

Vronsky watched Yuri hesitate, then climb in. Not good. Yuri wasn't the type to forget slights. His ledger ran deep, and one day there'd be a reckoning.

Vronsky shoved Keera into the back, climbed in beside her. Semyon paused at the intersection.

"Which way?"

"Vegas."

Semyon nodded and turned north.

"What about the old man?" Keera blurted. "He'll suffocate in the trunk."

Vronsky patted her knee. "It's okay. We're not animals. Before Semyon closed the trunk, he broke his neck."

CHAPTER 26

The sheriff's department was in Flagstaff, a forty-five-minute ride in the cruiser, all of it in silence. Lovejoy drove. Cooper sat beside Zach in the back. He clutched the water bottle the medic had handed him. The cops would follow their own interrogation rhythm—slow and thorough—while the Russians took Keera farther away.

Inside, Lovejoy left them. Cooper led Zach through a room of cubicles and busy deputies. At one desk, he booted up a computer.

"I need you to prove your ID," Cooper said.

"They took my wallet." Zach patted his pocket and produced a credit card. "All I got is this."

Cooper laid it on the desk and typed. "You keep this in a secret pocket or something?"

"Pretty much." He didn't elaborate—no need to waste precious time.

"Any other way of confirming who you are?"

"Try the *Chicago Post* website. There's a photo with my byline.

Bit dated, but still looks like me. Minus the bruises."

"Reporter, huh?" Cooper tapped at the keyboard. "Got yourself a story this time."

"Not by choice."

"Give me a description of the Russians."

"The driver—they call him Yuri. Flat face, flat blond hair. Thin, wiry."

"The hair or the body?" asked Cooper. He'd revealed a thinning top of his own when he removed his cap.

"The hair. He's slim but fit. Carries a weapon. They all do."

"What kind?"

"Dunno. The one I found was a Glock. They took it."

"Fine weapon."

"If you say so." Zach leaned back. "The main guy's Vronsky. He's the brains. Tubby around the waist, shortish. Long black hair to his shoulders."

"They speak English?"

"Vronsky and Yuri, yes, but accented. The other guy Semyon, can manage basic English."

"Describe him."

"Big. Bald—shaved. Hands like cinder blocks. Loves to use them. I could give a personal reference."

"Meaning?"

"He hit me."

Cooper paused his typing. "Guess you gave him a reason."

"Hey, I'm the victim here."

Cooper went back to the screen. "How do you know their names? Kidnappers don't usually introduce themselves."

"We overheard them. Names are easy to catch in a foreign language—they get repeated. They didn't hide much. Maybe they figured we weren't walking away."

He asked for Zach's home address and Keera's details.

"You have a photo of Keera Miles?"

"Give me Internet, I'll give you options." Zach opened his Facebook and scrolled. "Dark hair, any shot in the last six months—that's Keera."

Cooper led him to a gray, windowless interrogation room. One wall was a mirror. Deputies were probably watching from behind it. Another brought him coffee and a donut. Zach asked for more water. Got that too.

He wanted out. He needed Flint to contact him—and tell him where to find Keera.

Lovejoy entered, coffee in hand, and sat opposite, impassive.

"Nice room," Zach said.

"We like it," Lovejoy replied. He flipped open a pad and addressed the camera. "Detective Sergeant Franklin Lovejoy, date is August third, time is ten-oh-seven."

"Start from the beginning," he told Zach. "Leave nothing out.

"How's the hunt for the BMW?"

"No sign of it yet. Full name?"

"Zachary Bones."

"No middle?"

"My parents couldn't agree on one."

"Tell me your story."

"It'll take hours."

"We've got hours. Start talking."

So Zach talked. About Keera's disappearance. The psychic. The Russians at the apartment block. The clue to Sedona. Getting locked in the truck. The humiliating capture. The motel. Keera taken again.

Lovejoy: "Why'd they dump you and keep your girlfriend?"

"I don't know. It just happened that way."

Zach had interviewed enough people to know most didn't act rationally under pressure. Lovejoy probably knew it too.

"Bullshit."

"Maybe they killed the two guys over a dispute. I don't know. They knew I just wanted Keera. No beef with me."

"What two guys? I don't recall mentioning two guys."

Zach cursed himself. "Keera heard two shots. They were meeting the guy who hired them. I'm guessing he got it. And one other."

Lovejoy pounced. "You sound sure it was two deaths."

"Just a guess. Two shots, two bodies. How many were found?"

Lovejoy ignored the question. "Your story doesn't wash. They kidnap the girl. You find them twice. No cops. They let you overhear them, and then walk away. Doesn't track."

"I can't explain it either. They must've decided I wasn't worth the trouble."

"How long were you in the car?"

"About an hour."

"You hear the shots?"

"No. I got a text from Keera."

Lovejoy raised an eyebrow. "This gets better."

"It was a ransom demand."

"They wanted money from you?"

"They were sending a video to her father. Ransom details were coming."

"What kind of video?"

The worst I've ever seen, he wanted to say. "A video of her asking her father to follow instructions. Check my phone. It's not pleasant."

"Why did you get the message?"

"She used my number without them knowing."

"Why?"

"To buy time. To warn me."

"She know you were outside?"

"She didn't. She hoped I'd get the message and act."

"You think to call 911, or were you saving that for later?"

"I didn't want a shootout—with Keera in the middle. Thought I could stop them."

Lovejoy looked tired. "Where's your phone?"

"They left it. Bathroom floor. Out of reach. Said they'd call in a few hours to discuss the ransom."

Lovejoy scribbled something. "Can we call her phone? Reach them that way?"

"It's dead. They were looking for a charger."

"Make?"

"Samsung."

Lovejoy nodded. Zach leaned forward. "My phone is key. They think I've told you everything. They'll call."

"You'll make detective yet." Lovejoy studied him. "Is her father rich?"

"Never met him. But I guess he's got a few million. He's a Veep at an oil company."

Lovejoy sat up straight. "You know Bobby Flint?"

"Who?"

Exactly. The last person he could admit to knowing.

"Never you mind."

Zach shifted in his seat. "Can we move to the important stuff?"

"Which is?"

"They want me to contact her father. Arrange the money. They've left that to me."

"This is where we come in?"

"I hope so."

Lovejoy didn't buy it—not all of it—but he was listening. And if that meant a serious effort to find Keera, Zach could live with it.

"I don't know how to reach her father," he said. "You've got the demand, you've got me, and you've got evidence. Use it."

"His name?"

"Nelson Miles. As in my girl is many Miles away by now."

Lovejoy didn't smile.

"Isn't kidnapping an FBI thing? They'd know how to find him."

"You want to hand this off to the Feds?"

"I never said that. You acted fast. But there must be jurisdiction stuff here."

"Don't assume too much."

Cooper entered. "We found the SUV, sir. The second plate number matched. Vehicle was empty."

He paused.

"Except for the trunk."

CHAPTER 27

What was in the trunk," Lovejoy asked.

Not Keera, please not Keera. Zach willed himself to stay calm.

"A body. Old guy. In the Unity Church car park," Cooper said.

"In a churchyard? They swapped cars then," Lovejoy said, glancing at Zach. "An old man, damn. What was going on at the church this morning?"

"A wedding. Everyone's moved on to the reception. Minister said about a hundred attended—maybe fifty, sixty cars in the lot."

Lovejoy rubbed his chin. "Don't know why they killed the guy, but I'm sure it's his car they took. Get a description of the victim and send a couple of boys to the wedding party. We'll have to spoil the celebration. See if anyone matching that description was expected. Once we have a name, we'll run it."

"Yes, sir." Cooper left.

"Can I go now?" Zach asked. He needed quiet. Space. A chance for Flint to reappear. To give him Keera's whereabouts. Her condition. Jesus.

Lovejoy eyed him. "Explain why they left you alive, but killed someone who wasn't important to them."

"It's not logical, but it happened. Maybe they didn't want gun-shots at the motel."

"Still doesn't work for me, Bones. You're the only one—apart from your girlfriend—who can ID all three. They should've dumped you in the desert, full of holes."

"They got agitated when they realized you were coming."

"How'd they find that out?"

"The motel woman. When Yuri went to pay, he came back stressed. Said she was acting weird, and assumed you guys were on the way. They grabbed their stuff and bolted."

"But they left you behind."

"I think they wanted to travel light. But they weren't leaving Keera. Still a chance she leads to a big payout. I don't have the wealthy family she does."

"What's more likely is that you're in it with them."

The shift punched him in the chest.

"You're not serious."

Lovejoy leaned forward on his forearms. "Look at it from my point of view. Your girlfriend—rich daddy—disappears. She doesn't see you again until you pop out at Bobby's place. She can't verify anything before that. The Russkies go along with your version by holding you too. She doesn't know any better. You tell her to cooperate. You're their man on the inside. Very clever."

Fucking cops.

"This is about to go off the rails," Zach said. "You'll waste time checking my story while Keera—"

"None of it's true? Absolutely none?"

"Correct. Every word is a lie."

"They pressure her from without. You're the termite within."

"But I gave you descriptions. The plates. A hell of a lot more than you had. If I was working for them, why would I do that?"

"True. That's the only thing in your favor. The only thing stopping me from jamming you in the smallest box I have. You're a bothersome enigma, Bones. And I hate enigmas."

Zach exhaled. "What can I do to change your mind?"

"Go to a motel. Stay put until I say otherwise. You leave Flagstaff, I'll arrest you. You call the Russians, I'll hang you myself. Got that?"

"I can't call them. You've got my phone."

"Get another one. Leave the number with Cooper."

Lovejoy stood.

"You've got my credit card," Zach called after him.

A new deputy drove him downtown to a motel he pointed out. Handed back the card as Zach got out.

The motel was ritzy, spacious, and half the cost would be disallowed if he ever tried to expense it. Arched Spanish columns rendered in gray decorated the front. The fakery captured the colonial look but dispensed with the charm.

The desk clerk, a cheery Latina, flicked a startled glance at his face but said nothing.

"You have the finest mountain views in Flagstaff from your balcony in the morning," she promised, handing him his receipt and key card. "The sunsets are even better."

"I'll set my alarm," he said and rode the elevator up.

The mirror showed him a wreck. Wide-eyed. Hair greasy and defiant. He smelled like last night's garbage.

A shower revived him. Fresh clothes would finish the job—but they could wait.

"I need to buy a burner," he told the desk clerk when he returned. "And I need a computer with Internet."

"There's Wi-Fi in your room," she said. "And a phone store a couple blocks down the street. They rent computer time too. Turn left out of the motel. Easy parking."

"Thanks," he said, stepping out.

She expected him to drive two blocks? He soon understood why. The heat slammed down, bounced off pavement, and started caramelizing his skin.

He withdrew two hundred from an ATM and found the phone store just as his tongue turned into dry blotting paper.

A prepaid deal for $49. A wall of monitors. Backpackers emailing home. One free seat.

Two bucks for twenty minutes.

He opened a browser, searched for Vronsky's bank—Demir Bank of Kazakhstan. A Cyrillic jungle.

He shrank the screen and opened a Russian dictionary in a new window. Time bled away as he hunted the login button.

"You can have an hour for five bucks," the counter guy said.

"I'll take it."

The account number—eight digits Keera had given him—went in. The password was insultingly simple. CAWA1993. SASHA. The kid's name. 1993 must've been the birth year.

A new screen. Two options. He picked the highlighted one. More Cyrillic. He searched for the words meaning "account balance." Clicked.

A stream of numbers. The top row held all the excitement.

Vronsky possessed 3,005,746. US dollars.

He translated the account name—Sasha Investment.

The bastard had named it for his son.

He searched for "transfer," hunted through menus, cursed every banker who ever lived. Found the destination field.

Typed in his own Cayman account.

Three million dollars, out. Left the five grand. For Sasha's funeral. For flowers.

He memorized the keywords he'd translated in Google Translate. He might need to log back in later, especially if this next move failed.

The screen blacked out. He bought another hour. Checked his own balance. It had swelled from fifteen grand to over three million. The banks had removed about $250 in fees.

Now he had leverage. If they didn't release Keera, Vronsky lost more than he was asking in ransom. All Zach had to do was let them know.

They had Keera's phone. They'd find a charger. He'd call them. Explain about the money. Tell them to leave Keera somewhere safe. Great plan. One problem. If Lovejoy found out he'd made that call, he'd throw the book at him. The media too.

Three million dollars. Three million reasons not to be an idiot.

On the way back, he stopped at The Big Outside, a store filled with outdoor gear. A reedy clerk approached.

"Hi, can I help you?"

"Hiking pants. Lightweight. Three plain tees. Same number of socks and underwear."

"We've got changing rooms—"

"I trust your keen eye. You can see my size. Pile them on the counter and let me pay." With Keera still missing he didn't feel like checking out his ass in a mirror.

The clerk blinked, then got to work.

"These pants won't tear on the toughest cactus."

"They just need to cover my ass."

Silence. Bagged, folded, paid. Zach strode out.

Back at the room, he tossed the bag on the bed and plugged in the new phone. Two hours to full charge, but functional already. He showered again. The new clothes fit. He should've been nicer to the guy.

The bar fridge offered a water bottle and two paper-wrapped glasses. He ignored the beers and whiskies, and drank the water straight from the bottle.

The armchair faced the TV. He switched it on. News in five minutes. Five minutes to find out if Keera was alive.

Lovejoy's face appeared first, talking to cameras about two bodies found in a car. Not tourists. Not backpackers. A double homicide.

No mention of Keera.

An artist's impression of the three Russians followed. None accurate, but together—the big bald one, the skinny blond, the stocky long-haired guy—they were as distinctive as Larry, Moe, and Joe.

A local Chamber of Commerce rep insisted it wouldn't affect tourism. "We average two homicides a year. We've used up our quota."

Still no mention of Keera.

Zach turned off the TV. Took another drink. The whisper of the air conditioner was the only sound.

Then—a scratch.

Soft. Intermittent. He tried to ignore it. But it came again.

He raised his head. The wrapped glass was sliding across the countertop.

"Flint," he said. "About fucking time."

CHAPTER 28

Semyon barked an alarm: *"Mussor."*

Keera understood. Police.

Vronsky yanked her head down and shoved her into the Caddy's expansive footwell. He stretched out across the seats, pressing her neck flat in case she tried to rise.

Up front, Yuri dropped his seat to its lowest setting and slid out of sight.

They held the pose for a minute until Semyon muttered, *"Dobry."*

Vronsky slid off her, and she sat up again.

"Those two in the parked cruiser didn't even glance our way," Semyon said. "Kept looking behind us."

"Let's hope our luck holds," Vronsky muttered.

A few minutes later, Semyon took the I-40 ramp. They had a free run to Vegas—unless the old man was discovered too soon.

Keera hadn't expected this. Flint had warned her the Russians wouldn't buy Zach's secret-agency story. She hadn't told Zach—no point crushing his hope. It had been worth trying, if only to rattle them.

But this? Separated again?

She tried reaching out for Zach but couldn't calm her mind. No trace of him, no image, no feeling.

Bardo, she cried out silently. What do I do now?

No reply.

Still on her own.

Vronsky slumped in his seat. A botched job, the payout uncertain, these two idiots constantly at each other's throats—and Sasha dead. He should be beside his son's body, not stuck in America on a job gone sideways. He couldn't even grieve properly.

Fuck that. He'd finish the job in a day or two, however it played out, and go home. The money didn't matter anymore. There was always more.

But the girl. She and her boyfriend knew things they couldn't possibly know. Some of the guy's story was bullshit. But which parts?

How had they known Sasha was dead before he did? Sasha could've been killed only hours ago. A day, max. They knew names. Details. The boyfriend had found them twice.

Once, maybe. Some dreams gave insight. But twice? And no weapons? What government agency operated without weapons? Budget cuts didn't go that deep.

And the glass? Vronsky tried to force the data into a coherent theory. Nothing fit.

Yuri scrolled through his phone. "You want me to book ahead in Vegas?"

"Check small apartments," Vronsky said. "Places with lowlifes. Everyone minds their business. No one calls the cops."

"Lowlife, huh?" Yuri said. "Semyon will fit right in."

"Just find the right place," Semyon snapped. "You're the secretary. Do your job."

"This op isn't all muscle. Even a bonehead should get that." Yuri kept his voice level.

"You can go home early. Only girl left now."

"Even a small job, you'd fuck up."

"Gentlemen," Vronsky cut in. "We have many days together ahead. Try civility. Yuri, find a place. We'll go there."

Yuri glared at his screen, tension in his neck. That farm-boy fucker better be careful.

"Found one," he said. "Lots of complaints online. Shall I book?"

"You're shit secretary," Semyon muttered. "You want give cops time for ambush?"

"No booking," Vronsky said. "One of us goes in later, alone. The rest come after dark."

"How long we stay?" Yuri asked.

Semyon would stop whining fast if he lost an ear. And if he bitched, Yuri would take the other.

"They'll wait for contact," Vronsky said. "Give us time to surrender. But they don't know where we are. I don't buy the satellite crap. Not until we use the girl's phone."

The girl said, "I need a bathroom."

Semyon laughed. "Told you. She wants gas station restroom to leave message with woman inside."

Yuri turned to her. "We have two hours to go. Can you wait?"

"No," she said. "I can't."

Yuri turned forward. "Restroom's out. Go behind bush."

"I don't see any appropriate bushes."

Vronsky said, "Take next minor road. Out of sight from Interstate. Miss Keera will find suitable place, I'm sure."

Semyon exited five minutes later onto a new two-lane blacktop. No traffic. A dirt track veered right, vanishing over a rise. He followed it, stopped in the dip, turned around, and idled back to the top. The view stretched clear in both directions. The sun beat down like a sledgehammer. The ground looked like where dinosaurs came to die.

"Let's go," Yuri said to Keera.

She stepped from the car, slipped off her jacket.

Semyon stared.

Vronsky touched the door handle but jerked his hand back from the molten metal. The heat sucked the moisture from their skin.

Keera dropped her jacket on the seat and stretched, arms raised high, breasts lifting. Semyon didn't blink.

Stupid move, Yuri thought. Not with him watching. Not now.

Semyon shrugged off his jacket and placed it over hers. Deliberate. Keera's eyes met his. Blank. She gave nothing away.

"Come on," Yuri said, taking her arm.

"I'm coming too," Semyon announced.

"You want to watch her piss?" Yuri snapped.

"Better than watching you screw up."

Yuri said nothing. He yanked Keera forward, heading toward a mesquite ring.

"When she gets there, she strips," Semyon said.

Not a suggestion.

"We don't have time," Yuri said.

"I haven't had sex for three days."

Yuri stopped and faced him. "You're thinking with your dick while we're running from cops?"

"She's been teasing me."

He lunged. Caught her shoulder. Her dress tore.

She twisted, slipped free.

"Leave her!" Yuri shouted.

Semyon didn't stop. Just raised a middle finger.

Yuri stood, drew his weapon.

Two shots.

Semyon dropped to his knees. Yuri walked up and put a third in the back of his head.

Dust puffed.

"Go do your business," Yuri told Keera.

She didn't move. Just stared at the corpse, blood pooling.

"I changed my mind," she said.

Vronsky came running down the slope.

"What the hell did you do?" His voice rasped.

"He was going to rape her. We don't have time for that."

"You pulled your gun again? Like yesterday. What's with you? You turn into a cowboy?"

He stared at the body.

"The head shot? That was dumb. Now it looks deliberate."

"He was wasting time. We need to move."

Vronsky clutched his head like it might split apart. "We're short-handed now. That's why I hired both of you. How do you suggest we manage the girl?"

No answer.

He crouched, avoided the blood, and fished in Semyon's back pocket.

"We know where she lives and works," Yuri said. "If she gets away, we'll find her. Try for a payout again."

Vronsky pulled out a wallet, tossed it aside, and patted other pockets. Nothing. "Our faces are everywhere now. Border, airports."

"Vronsky," Yuri said. Then waited until Vronsky looked at him. "We've put two weeks into this. Sometimes it goes bad. You pivot."

"How do I explain this to his family?" Vronsky stood. "Police didn't shoot him. Two in the back. One in the head. Looks like an execution."

"It is a problem," Yuri admitted. "But we blame the secret agency."

"That nobody's heard of."

"That's why it's secret. Let's get to Las Vegas and reconsider our plans. We still have the girl, and once we have the charger, we have the father's number. We're still on course, we're headed in right direction."

Vronsky looked down at the body.

"We're headed somewhere, that's for sure."

CHAPTER 29

"Did I miss something?" A voice in Keera's ear. Flint. His form passed her, stopped at the spreading pool of blood.

"Oh my. The big fella bought it, did he? What a waste of human life. How did this happen?"

"Yuri got angry, shot him," she said, her words unspoken but transmitted. She left out the part where she'd teased Semyon to breaking point.

The idea had come from Bardo. Not all your assets are invisible, he'd said. It hadn't made sense at first, but she'd understood in the car—when Yuri was smoldering, just waiting for Semyon to screw up.

She'd seen it and took the chance. Maybe to fracture the group. Maybe to escape. But not this. None of this.

"Yuri loves his gun now," Flint said, picking up her thoughts.

"Where have you been?" she asked. "I thought you had a plan."

"Hey, lady, I got your boyfriend loose, didn't I?"

"You untied him?"

"Nope. Cops showed up, took him in for questioning, and guess what?"

"Don't, Flint. I'm wrecked. Just tell me."

He beamed like a kid. "That receipt I told you about? Cops found it. Matched it to your guy's story. Now they're hunting the Russkies."

"Where's Zach? Is he safe?"

"Oh sure. I watched him spin his tale. Detective didn't buy it."

"What does that mean?"

"He thinks your fella's working with them."

"For God's sake," Keera blurted aloud.

"The body disturbs you?" Yuri, hearing her disgust.

She drew a breath. "All of you disturb me."

Vronsky pointed at the body. He and Yuri hauled it up the slope and stuffed it in the trunk, leaving her at the bottom. No use running. Just alkaline desert and patchy scrub. No human could cross it without help.

"What are they thinking?" she asked Flint.

"Yuri's calmed down, but he knows he moved too fast. Now he's thinking of blaming the killing on Vronsky. Semyon didn't have many friends, but his family'll want payback. Better if they're hunting someone else."

"And Vronsky?"

"He's ahead of that curve. Knows Yuri's thinking it. Plans to kill him first."

"I'll be caught in a shootout?"

"Not here. That's all I know. You tell them about the bank account yet?"

She'd forgotten. "Has Zach done anything about it?"

"I'll say. Opened it. Took it all. Hope you trust a guy holding nearly three million bucks of Uncle Sam's cash."

"Three million?"

"Kidnapping pays, sweetheart. And remind your boyfriend—some of that money's mine."

Had Flint forgotten he was dead? "You want it back? In your condition?"

"I'd like it to go to a good home."

"No problem. I'll donate it to an environmental group."

Flint grinned. "You're a funny lady."

Up on the hill, Vronsky and Yuri stood by the car, their body language crackling with tension. Yuri opened the back door and jerked his head.

Keera didn't move. She beckoned Vronsky instead.

He paused, then descended the slope. "Still want a bathroom break?"

"We didn't get a chance to tell you one important thing," she said. "Your Kazakh bank account—ends in 3108. Password: Sasha1993. About three million U.S. in it."

His face didn't flinch, but she could feel the turmoil underneath. "You have no control over that money," she added. "It's ours now. Unless—"

"Not possible," he snapped—but there was doubt now.

Yuri slid down to join them. "What's she saying?"

"She knows my bank details," Vronsky said. "Maybe yours too."

"Bullshit."

"I'll check." Vronsky pulled out his phone, waited for a signal. Finally: confirmation.

"You took it," he said, staring at the screen. "You took it. I don't believe it." He looked again. "You left five thousand. Why?"

"Thought you'd need airfare home."

Zach had made a statement.

Vronsky looked up. "So we ask more for you now. To replace what you took."

It was the last swipe of a wounded tiger. They both knew it.

"We'll find wherever you stash your money," she said. "Again and again."

He glanced at Yuri. Her message had landed.

"What do you want?" Vronsky asked.

"Leave me in the next town. Take your chances with the cops. We won't interfere."

"Bullshit," Yuri spat. "She's bluffing."

"She had my bank access," Vronsky said. "Check yours."

Yuri pulled out his phone, tapped through screens. "Mine's fine. They only took yours."

Keera said, "You were next."

Yuri's mouth tightened. "We kill her and go. I move my money on the way."

"And we'll move it again. Can you hide it under your pillow tonight?"

"If we kill her," Vronsky said, "her agency kills us."

"If the boyfriend was telling the truth."

"She has my money. That's all the truth I need. We leave her."

"She'll walk back to the road and get help."

"How far to Vegas?"

"Less than an hour."

"How far back to the highway?"

"Three miles, maybe."

Vronsky checked the sun. High, hot, merciless.

"Sit down," he ordered.

"What for?" she asked, but obeyed.

"Feet out."

He yanked off one boot. Then the other.

"It's a long walk barefoot. By the time you reach the road, we're long gone. But we'll be back. In Chicago. Nothing is settled." He gestured to Yuri, and they climbed the slope.

"You're bad at this," Flint said. "You had them by the balls. Why not trade half the money for your freedom?"

"I just want them gone."

"Free? You're not free," Flint said. "You're barefoot in hell. Snakes and scorpions for neighbors."

"Do shut up. The worst reptiles are leaving."

Moments later, the Cadillac vanished, dust rising in its wake.

Keera stood. The ground scorched her bare feet. She knew it would only get worse.

"How far away are the police?" she asked.

"Not close. They'll ID the body in a couple of hours. By then, the Russians'll have a new car. Vegas and then..."

"You have to get Zach."

"How?"

"I don't know—text him, flash lights, spell it with glass—I don't care how. Just get him to me."

"No need to be grouchy," Flint said, and vanished.

She climbed the slope. The road unspooled into the shimmering heat, marked only by mesquite and dust. One dirt road. At least she could retrace their route.

She began walking, but within minutes knew she wouldn't make it.

Her pale skin stung like a swarm of bees settling on her

shoulders. She swallowed continuously to taste moisture, any moisture.

A tree alongside the road, its branches thin and gnarly, provided mediocre shade. She checked the ground for snakes and scorpions, asked Bardo to protect her, and sat under it, leaning against the trunk.

Semyon. No sense of him. Most of the dead didn't return quickly. Flint was the exception—tethered to his killers.

Zach. Could she reach him? Not yet. The sun pinned her to her body. No separation possible. Not now.

Maybe later, when it cooled.

She checked her watch. Ten-thirty. Hours to wait.

The heat climbed. She shifted with the moving shade.

They thought she'd reach the highway in a couple hours. They were wrong. She couldn't walk by day. Couldn't see by night.

She was trapped.

She hadn't had water since last night. Her organs had begun stealing moisture from her brain, shrinking it, igniting a skull-cracking headache.

She'd get light-headed soon. Confused. Might wander further into the desert, make a fatal mistake.

If she could walk. If she had days left.

I need water, she told Bardo. No reply.

Later: Please guide me to some, while I can still walk.

Nothing.

Rain would be good, she said as the sun reached its peak. Just a few drops. On my tongue.

By late afternoon the tree offered shade on the other side. She was too weak to move.

Help is sure to come, she thought. Today. Tomorrow. I just have to wait.

CHAPTER 30

A crunch of tires on the dirt road roused Keera. She opened her eyes. A battered green Ford pickup had stopped across from her. Engine running. The driver didn't move.

She tried to speak, but only a croak came out. She lifted a hand, then let it drop—the effort too great. Her bare legs burned, already lobster-red with sunburn.

"Help me," she whispered.

A door creaked. A woman crossed to her quickly. "Honey," she said, crouching, "I couldn't tell if you were dead or alive for a second."

She looked about fifty, no-nonsense in both tone and motion. Her hands gripped Keera's arms, pulling her up.

"Can you walk?"

Keera yelped as the woman's fingers touched scorched skin. They struggled to the pickup. Each step across the sunlit gravel sent daggers through her feet.

The woman gave her a shove from behind, helping her climb

in. Cold air blasted from the vents—inside the cabin, at least, the desert was defeated. The woman handed her a water bottle but Keera's fingers fumbled, couldn't grip.

"You're seriously gone," the woman said, and lifted the bottle to her lips.

Water cascaded down her throat, restoring a fraction of the energy the sun had drained. The woman touched the back of Keera's cheek, then aimed the AC vents straight at her glowing face.

"Let's get your temperature down fast."

She reached again for the bottle to pour water on Keera's head, but Keera grabbed it back.

"Okay, I get it." She pulled another bottle from the door pocket, unscrewed it, and dribbled water down Keera's head and neck. Dabbed her with a damp tissue.

"You need a hospital. How long were you out there? What happened? Car wreck? Are there others around?"

She didn't wait for an answer—just shifted the truck into gear and headed for the highway.

Keera shook her head. "It's only me." Her tongue thick in her mouth.

"Okay, honey. You're finding it hard to talk. I don't wonder. Just keep sipping that water. I'm calling an ambulance. Don't try to answer. Just letting you know."

She punched in 911. "I've found a woman with heatstroke. Taking her to the intersection of 79 and Interstate 40. Can you send help? She needs more than I've got."

She gave her plates and ended the call.

"You're lucky I was visiting my son. He's such a hermit, might not've driven out here for days."

She gave Keera a longer look. "You're not the hiking type, are you? Not dressed for it. No shoes, for heaven's sake. What happened?"

Keera faced the window. Couldn't talk. Didn't know how much to say.

"It's okay," the woman said. "You're disoriented. I can see that. I shouldn't be so talky."

I-40 came into view. The woman pulled over.

"We'll wait here. Ambulance'll be visible from a mile off."

They sat in silence, the AC cooling Keera's skin. She was free. Zach was free. They'd survived. The Russians were on the run.

It should've been over. But Vronsky had promised it wouldn't be.

Flint was having communication problems.

The glass slid on the counter, then stuck. The wrapping paper wasn't helping. Zach peeled it off, flipped the glass upside down, and tried again.

It slid freely now, gliding from end to end.

"You're trying to say something," Zach said. "Where's Keera?"

The glass moved two inches, then back. A yes.

"Okay, you want to talk." Zach rifled the hotel brochures, found a notepad, tore a page into quarters. On two pieces he wrote YES and NO, and placed them at opposite ends of the counter.

"Is Keera okay?"

The glass flew to YES.

"Can you take me to her?"

The glass hesitated, then moved away and stopped.

"Where is she?" Zach asked—then realized how stupid that

was.

The glass roamed like it was hunting letters.

"Okay, okay." He tore more pages, until the alphabet and numbers 0–9 were arranged in an oval.

"We're ready to rock," he said. "How far away is she?"

The glass nudged: 1…6…6.

"166 miles?"

YES.

"Toward Las Vegas?"

A pause, then YES.

"What road is she on?"

ON A ROAD.

"For God's sake. What fucking road?"

STAY POLITE ASSHOLE.

"Sorry. Stressful time."

APOLOGY ACCEPTED.

Zach exhaled, waited. The glass began moving again, slower this time, deliberate:

SILVER SPRINGS ROAD.

He grabbed his phone, typed it into Maps. There it was—tracing low hills along I-40.

"Long road you're sending me to, buddy. That's a two-hour drive."

Flint had advice about that.

DONT GO.

"What do you mean?"

IS SHE COMING BACK?

YES.

"The Russians bringing her?"

NO.

"Then what? Give me a straight answer."

ASK STRAIGHT QUESTIONS.

"Is she alone?"

SHE HAS A FRIEND.

A friend. Of course.

"Where is she going with this friend?"

TO HIGHWAY.

"Who's the friend?"

NOBODY YOU KNOW.

Christ.

NOT HIM.

Ha fucking ha.

"But a friend, right? I don't have to worry?"

NOT A HIM.

A woman, then.

"Was Keera released?"

YES.

Zach let out a breath. Russians gone. Keera free. Brought back by someone new.

"Where's she going?"

HOSPITAL.

Fuck. "You said she was all right!"

The glass skidded, letters flying.

SHE HAS SUFFERED.

Jesus.

HE CAN HELP BUT MEDICINE FASTER.

More jokes. Great.

Flint had placed her two hours away. Zach could be at the ER when she arrived.

"Will she be there soon?"

YES.

Zach grabbed his phone, reached for his keys—then stopped.

"Which hospital?"

The glass shot around again.

DONT GO.

"Why not?"

He was shouting at a glass.

CANT EXPLAIN.

"You can't explain? Why?"

YOU CANT EXPLAIN.

Then he got it.

As soon as Keera showed up, the hospital system would flag her. Missing person. Police would arrive within minutes.

And first question: How did you know your girlfriend was here? Russians tell you?

Lovejoy wouldn't buy Ouija board divination. Zach would be back in the box for days. Nothing in his story was verifiable. Even if the Russians were caught and vouched for him, no one would believe it.

Cops hated holes in their testimony—especially holes big enough to drive a Cadillac through.

"Thanks, Flint," Zach said aloud. "We'll talk again. Don't be a stranger."

The glass twitched left, then right. Stilled.

Zach tossed his phone and keys onto the bed. More waiting. Waiting for a deputy to give him news.

Hours to go.

Knowing the future wasn't all it was cracked up to be.

CHAPTER 31

Yuri parked the Cadillac at McCarran International Airport, Las Vegas.

"Get something plain with dark windows," Vronsky said, sliding out of the passenger seat.

Yuri stretched and strolled off down the rows, searching for the right car. Vronsky pulled their three packs from the back seat. He hesitated over Keera's boots and jacket but left them. Once Semyon's body was found, the girl and her boyfriend would be connected to him anyway. The clothes added nothing.

He wiped the steering wheel, dashboard, and door handles clean of prints with Semyon's spare shirt. Checked his bank account again. Still only five thousand dollars. Not a dream.

Yuri returned in a charcoal Honda and popped the trunk from inside. Vronsky loaded the packs and got into the back seat, handing over the Cadillac's exit ticket.

"You make me feel like taxi driver," Yuri half-complained.

"I don't want the motel guy to see two people."

Yuri entered the apartment address into the GPS and pulled

away. Vronsky stared out the window. Too hot for pedestrians; heat shimmered off parked cars.

At reception, Yuri dealt with the clerk while Vronsky stayed low in the tinted car.

"We're on second floor," Yuri said as they rolled into the parking garage.

The room was a time capsule—two beds (one a single), a sagging easy chair in dark brown fabric, and a crumbling television bolted above a counter.

They turned on the news. When Flint's car appeared onscreen, Yuri joined him.

"The discovery of two bodies in a car on the outskirts of Sedona has sparked a police search for three Russians who may be involved," the newsreader said.

A photofit image appeared—scratchy, but recognizably the three of them.

"It was mistake to leave boyfriend, eh?" Yuri said.

"It was a calculated risk. We needed him to facilitate the operation. But now things have changed."

Because of you, Vronsky wanted to yell. You and your need to pull out a gun to feel like a man.

"We had to move. But we can reach the girl again."

"You said she'd be better guarded now."

"I just need a few seconds with her. Maybe an email would work, but a face-to-face has more impact. I'll know if she believes me."

The news shifted topics. Vronsky turned off the TV.

"They've gone public. Because they have her. They won't expect us to contact them now."

"She already escaped desert?"

"Must have. They have surveillance somewhere—I'm sure of it. What kind? Who knows. But those two pulled off the impossible."

Yuri dumped the contents of his pack onto the bed. "I wouldn't have dumped her. She was our advantage. Our protection."

"You think it's easy to hide a hostage with only two men and keep moving? The plan was a snatch-and-hold. A few days, one place. This long haul needs more people."

"We should've discussed it. Debated."

"While cops were hunting the Cadillac?" Idiot. Promoting himself to strategist now?

"You reacted to the money. You didn't see the bigger picture."

"It wasn't your money," Vronsky snapped.

"You have other accounts, I'm sure."

"True. But that was the main one. And I owe people for setting this up."

"Pay them from what we've got."

"After expenses, we have three hundred thousand. We owe them two."

"But deal fell through."

"You think they care? They agreed to wait only because they know me. Normally it's upfront. I still have to pay. If I don't give them silver, they'll give me lead. Then come for you."

Yuri nodded. "We have problem. I'll think of something. Leave it to me."

Like you thought of shooting Semyon, Vronsky thought. What an act of madness.

"First, we change our clothes. Something more colorful, new season's fabrics and styles. Blend in with the tourists."

"Pick something. Large size for me."

"Give me a thousand for clothes. Then we can split the rest."

Vronsky pulled a white envelope from his pack, peeled off a few bills, and handed them over.

"Get the clothes. By the time you're back, money's sorted, Semyon's things ready for disposal, and we'll have a new plan. We split up soon. Bring scissors and clippers—I need a new look."

Surprisingly, Yuri didn't argue. He swapped his black tee for a blue-and-white striped shirt, tucked his gun into his waistband, and pulled the shirt down over it.

"There's a big mall nearby. Saw it on the GPS. Might take a while. Just because it's a disguise doesn't mean I drop standards."

"Whatever you want, fashion guru."

"I think Hawaiian shirt for you. Calf-length shorts."

"*Bozhiyei Materi*, you tell anyone I wore that, I kill you."

Yuri laughed. "When you're not looking, I'll take photo with phone."

"I'm always looking. Don't even think about it."

When Yuri left, Vronsky changed into fresh clothes.

His money. If they wanted to keep the girl safe, they'd return it—with interest. He'd deliver the message personally. And if the boyfriend was there? Shoot him. A quick conversation, then a bullet.

Cleaner than kidnapping. No hostages. Just cause and consequence.

He packed his bag again, stuffing the leather jacket in. Opened the envelope one last time. Flint's coffee money—still the full hundred grand. He pushed it into his jeans pocket.

He pulled his hair back, twisted it tight, and jammed it under a cap. Slung the pack over his shoulder, grabbed his phone, and left.

On the street, heat bounced off the pavement like a punch. in the face. He walked fast to the used car dealership he'd seen earlier.

Ten minutes later, slick with sweat, he entered the show-room.

"Hi there," said a salesman. "Looking for anything specific?"

Vronsky pointed to a silver Lexus out front. "How much for that?"

"Got a trade-in?"

"No. I've got cash. I want to leave soon. Can you make it happen?"

"Just a minute, sir."

The salesman hustled to an office and spoke with another man. Returned smiling.

"It's three years old—asking twenty-five. For cash, we can do twenty-two."

"That's good. I leave in ten minutes with the car."

"Paperwork takes a bit longer, sir," he chuckled, patronizing. Vronsky dropped his pack, pulled out the envelope. The bills were in five-thousand-dollar stacks. He separated five and held them up.

"You bring keys and papers. Show me where to sign. I give you twenty-five. You keep the paperwork. I'll call you later with an address to send it. You have ten minutes. In eleven, I'm gone."

He sat and checked his watch. Didn't look up.

The salesman returned in seven minutes. Three minutes later, Vronsky was on the road.

As he merged into traffic, he dialed 911.

"Flagstaff sheriff," he told the operator.

He was transferred.

"You're looking for two Russians? Room 207, Sunlight Resort, Las Vegas. If it's empty, sit and wait. They're out shopping."

He ended the call. Switched off the phone and dropped it on the passenger seat.

He'd wait for Yuri's arrest to hit the news. Then call Russia. Tell them who killed Semyon. The girl had seen it. No one would doubt him.

Yuri would be safer in jail. For a while.

The girl and boyfriend would stay in Flagstaff a few days. She was probably in the hospital. Americans needed medication for everything—too much sun, too much snow. Weaklings.

The boyfriend would stay close. They'd tell their story again and again to police. They'd have to identify Yuri.

It bought him time.

Two days. Maybe more.

He took the I-15 turnoff, accelerating as he merged with traffic. A green road sign loomed ahead, destinations in white.

Only one mattered.

Chicago 1700 miles.

CHAPTER 32

Zach opened his door to hard knocking. Lovejoy stood outside, flanked by two deputies. He was unhappy, like a grizzly type of unhappy.

"You didn't call in with your new number," he said.

"I couldn't. Had to charge the phone first."

"You could've used the motel phone."

"I forgot. I was worried about Keera. And the call—from the Russians. Did they make it?"

Lovejoy ignored the question. "What's the number?"

Zach gave it to him.

"Have you found her?" he asked.

Lovejoy jotted the number down. "When I call, you'd better answer. If you don't, I'll have you for obstruction of everything that's good in this country."

"I will. I will, okay? But Keera—what do you know?"

He paused, then gave a little ground to professional courtesy.

"We found your girlfriend dumped in the desert, near the interstate to Vegas. She was in bad shape from the heat. She's in hospital now, recuperating."

"Where? What hospital?" Zach started toward the door, but Lovejoy blocked him.

"She'll survive. But she's not fit to talk. Mostly incoherent. Your lovers' reunion can wait. I have more information if you want it."

The two deputies stood in the doorway, chewing gum behind their dark shades.

"Can you fill me in on the way?"

"Nope."

"You catch the Russians?"

"No. But there's only two left."

"How come?"

"One of them's dead."

"Who?"

"A big fella."

Semyon.

"Who killed him?"

"Ms. Miles says it was Yuri."

Jesus. Two dead this morning alone. Keera must've witnessed it. Maybe both. The trauma, on top of the sunburn—she wouldn't just be dehydrated, she'd be wrecked.

"I have to see her. Tell me where she is, or I'll search every fucking ward in every city in the state."

Lovejoy studied him for a full minute.

"I'm not convinced I have the whole story. I don't know if I'm chasing two kidnappers or if all five of you conspired to extract money from Nelson Miles."

"Did you talk to him?" Zach had forgotten about Keera's father. "Is he coming here?"

"Like any doting father, he can't believe his darling would do anything wrong. He's spoken to her and is relieved it ended without harm. He'll be here in the morning. His people will be here tonight."

Lovejoy pulled a small notebook from his pocket. "Their names are Hancock and Brooks. Sound like lawyers."

"You tell him about Flint yet? That he was involved?"

"That's the interesting part, Bones. And the only reason you're still sitting in comfort and not somewhere less so. Flint's company was bidding on a construction and maintenance contract that Miles's corporation had out. Maybe he tried to swing it by holding the Miles girl. Shit went sideways, and Flint got killed. Judging from the video on your phone, the Russkies decided to carry on alone."

"Has the kidnapping hit the press yet?" Zach remembered the noon bulletin—just the car, no mention of abduction.

"No," Lovejoy said. A vein bulged in his forehead. "We kept it simple. Just a hunt for suspects in Bobby Flint's murder. Now Nelson Miles is talking to my superior. He doesn't want the kidnapping mentioned. Says if people hear how easily she was taken, it might give others ideas."

Lovejoy looked like he'd just been ordered to swallow cockroaches.

For all his bluntness and aggression, the sergeant seemed like a real cop. One who wanted the truth—just the truth. But the truth, Zach knew, was a fragile thing. One whisper from the right corner, and the whole case could vanish.

He tried to lighten the mood. "Well, that thins your caseload."

Lovejoy didn't smile. "You gonna write this up? Make us look like dummies?"

"Hardly. If the kidnapping never happened, I don't have a story."

"They got to you too, huh?"

Zach heard the disgust. In another time, he might've called this man a soul mate. Not now.

"Nobody got to me. But it's in nobody's interest to make waves here."

"Sure it isn't," Lovejoy sneered. "Marvelous what money can buy."

No comeback to that. It was what had always driven him—to uncover corruption in Chicago. And now he was part of the same devil's pact.

"I don't want to think about it."

"Flagstaff Medical Center," Lovejoy said finally. He looked tired.

"Go see your girlfriend. But don't leave the county without my say-so."

The deputies stepped aside. Lovejoy left. They didn't close the door.

A deputy sat in a chair outside Keera's room. He stood up, hand outstretched.

"This is a no-go area, buddy."

"I want to see Keera. We were abducted together."

The deputy sized him up. Realization dawned.

"Detective Lovejoy said you could have two minutes. ID?"

Zach showed his credit card.

"That all you got? Don't drive?"

"I was abducted. The Russians took everything else. Lovejoy sent me. Call him if you want—he's in a real cheerful mood."

The deputy handed the card back as a nurse arrived.

"He's got two minutes," he told her.

She nodded like that made perfect sense, then entered the room. Zach followed.

Keera was asleep. A tube in her arm. Another under the blanket. She looked soft and small, her dark hair spread like a halo on the pillow, hands tucked under her chin.

The nurse whispered, "Don't wake her. She needs rest, not stress. She'll be fine soon. We're replacing the sugars, salts, and electrolytes she lost..."

Maybe realizing Zach wasn't after a medical lecture, she stepped back.

He stared at Keera. Wanted to hold her. Settled for stroking her hand.

It wasn't nearly enough.

He left. The nurse closed the door behind them.

"There's a waiting room for friends and family." She pointed down the hall.

The couch was already occupied by a large woman stretched the length of it. He sank into a hard chair and tried to process the day.

Two Russians still out there. Vronsky wouldn't forget the three million. He'd come for it. He knew where to find Keera.

This time would be different. It would be money or blood.

At least they were warned. He had to find a way to stop them.

They had guns. He had a press pass.

He was dozing when a hand rested on his shoulder. He blinked up into dark eyes and a finely tailored suit.

Another suit stood behind him.

"Good evening," the first one said. "I'm Hancock. This is

Brooks. We work for Prime Resources. We need to confirm who you are."

"Zach Bones," he said, dragging himself upright. "Keera's partner."

"ID?"

He fished out his credit card. Hancock glanced at it.

"This all you have?"

"The Russians took the rest."

Hancock nodded. "We know about you. The nurse will find you a room. If Miss Miles asks for you, I'll come get you."

Zach looked him over. "Your ID?"

Hancock handed over a business card: *Bryan Hancock, Prime Resources.*

"This all you got? You could've run this off at Kwik Kopy."

Hancock and Brooks exchanged a glance. Hancock sighed and produced a driver's license.

"You've gained weight since this was taken," Zach said. "You should be more careful at your age."

"Thanks for the advice."

Zach gestured down the hall. "You two going to stand guard with the cop? I'm not being flippant. These Russians have killed four people in twenty-four hours. You'd better be armed."

Hancock's eyes widened slightly. News to him.

"We'll be ready."

The nurse returned. "There's a room for friends and family— number 511. It's yours. The bill's been covered."

"Thanks."

Zach found it, fell onto the bed without undressing.

He pictured Keera with tubes in her arm. The three million in his account. Mostly, he pictured Vronsky coming for them.

Again.

CHAPTER 33

Yuri took two hours to decide on his purchases but had no doubts about any of them. For himself, Polo tops and Ralph Lauren pants. Stylish but not flashy —made him look successful. He eyed Italian labels but decided they'd look out of place here.

For Vronsky, he picked Tommy Hilfiger and chuckled. When Vronsky put it on, he'd tell him that was the brand worn by Blacks and Asians in America. Too late for him to do anything about it. That thought made Yuri laugh even more. He bought two caps as well. One said NY, the other SOX.

Back at the apartment building, he pulled into the underground garage and reached into the back seat for his parcels.

Quick footsteps echoed on the concrete. Before he could turn, a hand shoved his head down onto the seat and cold metal pressed against his neck.

"Police," a voice snapped. "Don't move."

More hands grabbed his wrists, yanked them behind his back. Nylon cuffs zipped tight around them. He was hauled upright and shoved against the wall.

He glimpsed a cop standing a few feet away, both hands on a chest-level gun, aimed right at him. Another officer patted him down, pulling the gun from Yuri's waistband. His wallet followed into a plastic evidence bag.

"Where's your buddy?" someone asked.

"What is going on? Am I parking in the wrong position?"

"We got a wise guy," the voice rasped. "Excuse us if we don't laugh. Where's your buddy?"

"What is buddy?"

Vronsky must have gone out. Just his luck.

"How long you been in America that you don't know what a buddy is?"

Yuri stayed silent.

"Read him his rights. Let's move. He'll stall all night—I know the signs."

"Stake out the garage?" another officer asked.

"Yeah. They might've ditched the Caddy, but they could have another car."

Two cops flanked Yuri and led him to an unmarked vehicle. They shoved him into the back, and one slid in beside him.

Two hours later, with the paperwork finally squared away, a patrol car barreled down I-40 toward Flagstaff. Yuri stared at the plastic-covered seats and wondered if they'd been cleaned. Who'd ridden back here before? What had they done?

At the station, fresh officers escorted him to an interrogation room. It smelled like bleach and bad decisions.

A big man filled the doorway.

"I'm Detective Sergeant Franklin Lovejoy, Sheriff's Department," he said, lowering himself into the chair opposite. "Your shopping was interesting. You had several changes of clothing—in two sizes."

"I don't understand American measurements. So I bought extra," Yuri said.

"You could've tried them on."

"Dressing rooms very shabby. Not enough mirrors to show off all sides."

Lovejoy nodded slowly. "I can understand that. You seem like a fastidious guy. You like to make a good first impression."

Yuri inclined his head, accepting the compliment.

"I'm wondering why you carry a gun."

"America is dangerous. People jump on you in parking garages."

"We only do that when we've got a good reason."

"For what reason did your people jump me?"

Lovejoy ignored the question. "You have a gun permit?"

"In my luggage. Unless the police stole it. I hear there's much corruption in America."

"The gun. Where'd you get it?"

"From a friend. I was worried about Vegas crime rate."

A deputy entered and handed Lovejoy a note. The detective read it and looked up.

"We found your friend."

"I have many. Which one?"

"The one you shopped for groceries with. His body was found in a Cadillac in Vegas."

"Really?" Yuri paused. "Crime rate worse than I thought."

Lovejoy didn't laugh. "What was your friend's name?"

"Baldy."

Lovejoy leaned forward, bracing his hands on the table like he was anchoring it—and himself.

"You don't seem very shaken by the news."

"I've learned to keep my feelings private. It's undignified to weep and wail in public."

"Was Baldy the man who gave you the gun?"

"No. That was another friend."

"Can you tell me his name?"

Yuri shook his head. "I don't want trouble for him. He's a nice person."

Lovejoy stood. "We'll talk again. Real soon."

Back in his cell, Yuri sat on the edge of the cot, staring at the wall. Had they caught Vronsky, too?

No. They'd be playing that card—saying Vronsky's story didn't match his, saying Vronsky blamed him for everything.

That was the game. Make you doubt your own side.

So if they hadn't caught Vronsky... then he never came back. Which meant...

He'd taken off. Left him behind. Back to Chicago. With all the money. Yuri felt heat crawl up his neck and across his scalp.

Vronsky had sold him out.

CHAPTER 34

Zach woke to the door crashing open—and a female figure launching herself at him. Keera.

She clutched him tightly, burying her face in his neck. He wrapped his arms around her and stroked her hair.

"You're okay, then," he said, grinning like a kid on Christmas morning.

"Mmm," she murmured, nuzzling closer. Then she lifted her head and kissed him all over his face.

"The desert air agrees with you," he said, savoring this rare burst of affection. "We should camp out more often."

She laughed and pulled him upright. "Let's eat and talk."

Brooks was outside, watchful. "The cafeteria is this way," he said.

Zach followed him, inspecting Keera as they walked. Her face was sunburned but not blistered. The hospital robe masked the rest, but her energy was back. That's what happens when your chakras realign, he supposed.

At the cafeteria, Brooks showed them to a table and joined

Hancock at the next one. Keera shot them a glare, and they moved further away.

"They're watching out for me," she said. "Not eavesdropping."

Zach brought coffee for himself, herbal tea for her, and toast for both. "You look radiant. In both senses of the word," he said. "How are you feeling?"

"Better than I expected. My legs are cherry red, sting like hell when the cream wears off. But otherwise fine." She sipped her tea and made a face.

"I thought I'd lose my mind, worrying. Thank God Flint showed up with his glass trick and told me you were okay."

"He did that? He's getting more human."

She reached out and touched his cheek. "I'm so sorry I put you through this."

"You didn't. The Russians did."

"There's only one left," she said. "The police picked up Yuri. He went shopping instead of staying on the run."

"Only Yuri?"

"A Russian-sounding guy called the sheriff's office, told them where to find him. I haven't heard the tape, but I'm sure it was Vronsky."

"He shafted him? Hard to believe." He shook his head. "This changes things. In our favor."

"You weren't with them long. Yuri and Semyon hated each other, that was clear, but Vronsky didn't care for either. He needed them. But when Yuri shot Semyon, it shattered the group."

For someone who'd just witnessed two murders, she seemed... fine. Smiling. Vibrant.

Still, he had to ask. "You really okay? You saw people die. Right in front of you."

Her face shuttered. "I coped. It's easier when you know life isn't permanently extinguished. With Semyon, I was glad he was gone. Brutal, but quick." She shrugged and picked up her tea again.

It was a front, he was sure. But she'd shut the door, and he knew better than to push at it.

He switched topics. "What about Vronsky? Are we still in danger?"

She shook her head. "No closure until he's caught. He's coming back to finish the deal."

"He told you that?"

"Yes. And I got an image—he's driving to Chicago. He'll be there before us."

"What?" He sat back. "We're walking into an ambush?"

"It's not an ambush if we know it's coming."

"If we don't know where or when, it's still an ambush. Anything else you want to share?"

"Nothing comes to mind. Give me time to settle my soul back into my body—I'll know more then."

She said it so calmly, he let it go. For now.

"Seen your dad?"

"He was here earlier." Her smile came too quick. "Very concerned. Told his men to fix my security. Make my place bombproof."

"He's gone already?"

Her eyes flicked away. "He said he had urgent stuff. He knew I didn't want him hanging around, patting my back."

The way she said it made Zach think that's exactly what she'd wanted.

He squeezed her hand. A gesture of sympathy. She responded with a flash of ice. Her signal: Stay out of my emotional space.

"Does he know about me?" he asked.

"The basics," she said, waving a hand.

"The cops thought I was working with the Russians. Did you tell him that's impossible?"

"He knows I trust you. He'll follow my lead."

I bet he will, Zach thought. It'd take a brave man to give Keera advice.

"What are the cops doing about your kidnapping?"

"You were kidnapped too, remember? They're doing nothing. They've got enough on Yuri and Vronsky for the murders. No one wants to complicate things with extra charges. Daddy convinced them to leave it out."

"I'm sure he did." His voice was flat.

She stiffened. "I know what you're thinking. But if the story gets out, it could inspire more kidnappings of executives' families. Let's leave it there."

"I know. I get it. It still grates—the rich get to rewrite events. The rest of us can't."

"You would if you could."

"Probably. But I'd feel bad about it."

"At least Lovejoy's off your back," she said. "He connected Flint to my father. That's taken the heat off you."

Zach nodded toward the guards. "How long are Rocky and Bullwinkle sticking with us?"

"They'll escort us to Chicago. Stay for a week or two while my house gets tricked out with every security measure known to man. Then I'll turn most of it off. I'm not a caged bird."

"You're definitely not."

He kissed her. To his surprise, she lingered before pulling away.

His sins, it seemed, were forgiven.

"Where's Vronsky's money?" she asked.

"Resting happily in my Cayman account."

"And...?"

"And what?"

"What are your plans for it?"

"Plans? I will use it to fight evil." He grinned. She wasn't smiling.

"You can't keep it."

"You want me to give it back?"

"No. But some deserving cause—there must be one."

"The most deserving cause I see is me."

"I can't believe you're saying this." She slapped the table. "Give it away."

Hancock and Brooks looked over.

"You want me to give away three million dollars? That'd take a lifetime to earn. This money frees me. And, for the record, half is yours."

"I don't want dirty money earned through death."

"Money doesn't have guilt."

"Give it away."

"Easy for you to say. You've got a trust fund. I bet you've got more than three million coming your way."

She said nothing.

"Easy to sneer at money when you've always had it. Try living without it."

"I get your point, Zach, but—"

"It's offshore. I can't bring it into the U.S. without triggering alarms. The Feds would hit me with charges I've never heard of. They'd ask where it came from, where it's going. If they think it's tied to terrorism, I'm finished. I need coffee."

He fetched another cup and a glazed donut. "I need a sugar hit," he said, biting in as she watched with disapproval.

"We could donate it anonymously," she said.

"Sure. So it can buy new cars for the charity execs. That'd drive me nuts."

She sighed and bit into her toast—plain, no butter. "You plan to leave it offshore forever?"

"We could take a few trips to the Bahamas."

"Not an option," she said mid-chew.

He shrugged. "I don't know what to do with it. But something will come to me."

"Flint thought it might be smart to offer Vronsky half. Buy him off."

Zach considered it. "You think he'd stick to a deal?"

"He was shell-shocked when we emptied his account. I told him we could do it again. He believed me. He'd take any deal seriously."

So this was where they were—negotiating with a killer.

"Then we'd be no better than a store owner paying protection. And what stops him from asking for more?"

She stayed silent. Agreed, it seemed.

Zach drained his coffee and clattered the cup into the saucer. "We have to intercept Vronsky. Neutralize him."

She stared. "Neutralize him? Are you saying what I think you're saying? Is this masculine pride talking?"

"Maybe. But I won't live my life looking over my shoulder. He's coming—you said so. This time, we'll be ready."

CHAPTER 35

C ooper appeared in the cafeteria before they'd finished breakfast. That he wore a deputy's uniform
didn't stop Hancock and Brooks from rising to intercept him.

"You know this man?" Hancock asked Keera, planting himself in front of Cooper. Brooks stood close enough to grab an arm
if necessary.

"I do. He's a deputy, like the uniform says," Zach said while the
two guards engaged in a stare-down.

"You don't know what a deputy looks like?" Cooper asked
Hancock. "You grow up in China?"

"It could be a fake," Hancock replied, dismissive.

Cooper scowled and turned to Zach and Keera. "Detective
Lovejoy wants you two to come with me to the holding cells. We
need you to ID the Russian suspect we've got. Also, photos of the
guy found at Vegas airport."

"I need more clothes than a dressing gown," Keera said.

"We'll bring Miss Miles and her friend," Hancock said. "We'll be there by lunch."

"No later," the deputy replied, like he was assigning home-work.

They stopped at the same store where Zach had bought his clothes. The clerk remembered him and nodded warily, saving his greeting for Keera.

She moved quickly through the racks, emerging from the dressing room in dark green bush pants and a gray tee, clutch-ing a lightweight hiking jacket. She paused at the counter to at-tach turquoise and silver Navajo earrings. They set off her sun-flushed face perfectly. Hancock paid.

At the sheriff's office, Lovejoy took them to a room with a wall-mounted monitor. The feed cycled through six holding cells—six men, same ending. Jail.

"That's Yuri," Keera said, pointing. "He shot Semyon. Saved me from rape."

What? She hadn't told him that.

"We're focusing on Bobby Flint's murder, like I said," Lovejoy replied. "Your desert adventure is unrelated."

She glanced at Zach. "Yes, I understand."

Lovejoy raised an eyebrow at Zach.

"Yes, that's him," Zach said. "The one they called Yuri."

"You'd swear to that in court?"

"I want these guys locked up forever. Don't treat me like one of them."

Lovejoy grunted. Zach asked, "Don't you usually use a one-way mirror? This feels... casual. Low-res, too."

Lovejoy didn't answer. He led them back to his office, pulled an eight-by-ten photo from a file, and slid it across the desk.

"You recognize him?"

Zach studied the ruined face of Semyon. Even with the exit wound, it was unmistakably him.

"It's the big bastard," Zach said. The image of that massive hand smashing Keera's face returned. "Yes, I'll testify."

"Semyon," Keera said, then looked away.

Lovejoy switched on a recorder. Vronsky's voice poured from the speakers.

"You recognize him?" he asked.

"Vronsky," Keera said.

"It's Vronsky," Zach agreed. "He sounds helpful."

"He's dumped his friend," Lovejoy said, shutting off the recorder and leaning back.

"What?"

"We've got enough to charge Yuri with Flint's murder and Semyon's. Same gun, ballistics match, GSR on his clothes. He's made this easy."

Lovejoy didn't sound pleased.

"Glad to hear it," Zach said. "Your case folder's almost wrapped. One fugitive left."

"We've got more than that to clean up," Lovejoy muttered. "We're treating Miss Miles' discovery in the desert as unrelated —an unexplained abduction. No robbery, no assault, and the victim was released unharmed. No resources allocated."

"Sounds reasonable," Zach said. "What about me? The motel woman saw me."

"She's the only one. You're practically a phantom. But we saw you—tied to the sink. My favorite memory of you."

Some people didn't even try to be friends.

"She won't talk to the press?"

"I spoke to her," Lovejoy said bitterly. "She doesn't want her motel in the news. Can't recall seeing you at all."

"So you don't need me or Keera for the trial?"

"Correct. But I had to be sure we had the right guys. We'll try Yuri on forensics alone."

"You'll try? Not enough to convict?"

Lovejoy gave him a look that could curdle blood.

"You two are my best witnesses, crucial witnesses. Your testimony would close the case minutes after it opened. But now, you don't exist. By royal fucking decree. The rest of the evidence is only circumstantial, just might be leaky enough for a good lawyer to spring Yuri. And Vronsky, if we catch him."

He drained a glass of water. "If those two walk, you're both in mortal danger. Anybody think of that before sticking their two cents in?"

Zach couldn't argue. Lovejoy painted a picture a blind man and his dog could recognize. While Yuri and Vronsky lived, he and Keera couldn't sleep. And the law had no answers.

"It didn't work out how it should've," Zach said. "But I didn't steer it that way."

Lovejoy spread his hands and stared at them. "What I know is, those with power interfered in police work. I have to accept it. I don't have to like it." He raised his eyes. "And I don't have to like those who benefit from it."

"I didn't lie to you," Zach said.

"Get out of my county, Bones. We used to have the rule of law around here. You and your kind are tearing it down."

Yuri rattled his cell door. A deputy appeared.

"You looking for trouble?" he asked. "We like it quiet."

"I want to speak to legal representative. Please bring phone."

The deputy gave him a long look, then returned with keys. "You still want it?"

Yuri nodded. The cop opened the door, cuffed him, and led him to a wall phone. Two deputies typed on keyboards nearby. No one looked like they were listening—but only an idiot would assume that.

"I get privacy?"

"You get five minutes."

"But this is private conversation with lawyer. I need to tell family, also, where I am."

"You've got four and a half."

Yuri dialed a New York number"It's me," he said in Russian. "I don't have much time. Send our legal guy. I'm in Flagstaff, Arizona. Sheriff's Department."

"I thought you were in Chicago."

"Arizona."

"They charge you?"

"No one's read charges, but they're talking murder. Must be a mistake."

"Definitely. You are a sweet and gentle person. A lawyer will be on way to you this hour. Anything else we can do?" The voice tight with suppressed curiosity, but restrained from talking too much over a phone call.

"My associates," Yuri said. "Baldy's dead, the other's disappeared. Can you locate him?"

"Is he returning to New York?"

"No, other place."

"It's done."

"*Spasibo*." Thanks.

He hung up and caught movement from the corner of his eye.

For one second—just one—he saw Flint standing beside him.

He whirled. No Flint. Just the deputy, jingling keys.

"You nervous?" the deputy said. "I'd be jumpy too."

Yuri said nothing. The deputy returned him to the cell and locked it.

"It's lunch soon. You have menu?"

"You got Quarter Pounder with fries. Eat it or flush it. Your choice." The deputy walked off before Yuri could respond.

Lovejoy came later. "Your lawyer's on the way?"

"Not yet. But he's coming." Yuri said. "You know how top people are. Busy, busy, all the time."

"Get yourself someone who cares more. We're moving you after lunch. To Phoenix. That's where you'll be until the murder trial."

"You have your duties," Yuri said with a shrug.

Lovejoy left. Yuri leaned back, thinking.

He played over his conclusion that Vronsky had turned him over to the cops. Maybe he'd been hoping for a shootout with no Yuri left to tell his story. The truth would come out soon enough. Vronsky wouldn't last long if he returned to Chicago.

Cops. They only talked of the killing. They were ignoring the kidnapping, never asked about the boyfriend.

He swung around on the bench and lay down, his hands under his head. Did the girl and the boyfriend tell them about this secret organization? If they had, the cops might get instructions to leave out any evidence of those two being involved.

He sat up. He'd get off; he knew it now. If not totally, then a token sentence, with early release. There was no other way of figuring it. He could blame Semyon for Flint's death and the old man's death, and blame Vronsky for Semyon's death. The cops could ignore evidence to the contrary if they wanted to.

All around the world, they did that when it suited them.

He might not serve any major time. A few weeks in jail while his lawyer plea-bargained, out on bail when it became clear his charges wouldn't be so serious. Then back to Mother Russia.

Kiss this country goodbye.

He stood, rattled the door, and yelled, "Where's my Quarter Pounder?"

Vronsky calculated: thirty hours of driving, two sleep breaks. The road through Nebraska was a long, cracked ribbon. Trucks both ways. Rocky scrub on either side.

He called Moscow.

"We have situation," he said. "Yuri went mad. Shot Semyon."

"He wanted all the money?"

"There is no money. Project collapsed. Cops came. I escaped."

"Why did he shoot Semyon?"

"Personal. He denied it. Said Semyon was endangering the operation."

"What do you want?"

"Tell Semyon's people. The killer is in custody in Flagstaff, Arizona. They'll move him soon."

"They can move him to Fort Knox." The voice laughed. "He'll still be found."

"Tell them. He'll try to blame me, but ballistics don't lie."

"What now? You coming home?"

"Airports are risky. I'll go to Canada or Mexico first. I'll call again."

He hung up. Next billboard: Chicago, 1100 miles. He had to sleep soon, or he would end his life wrapped around a roadside boulder, a momentary sideshow for those passing. His eyes were scratchy with grit, the morning sun warming his chest, bringing on dangerous drowsiness.

He needed sleep. Not a motel—too risky. A parking garage would do. An hour's rest, then back on the road.

The kidnapping—simple at first. One girl. Four days. A million bucks.

Now? Total chaos.

He'd find her again. Watch her house. Then deliver the message: the money back in 24 hours. Plus one million more. No guards could stop a sniper or a car bomb.

Her father would understand.

And Sasha... dear God, Sasha.

He barely got to know his son before the powder took him. The funeral was in a week. He'd be there. Find out who supplied the stuff that destroyed him. Remove the bastards from the earth, a small piece at a time. Something to look forward to.

He slowed and exited the highway.

CHAPTER 36

Zach knew Keera wouldn't take the news well. He let Hancock start.

"The doctor says you need another twenty-four hours of observation," Hancock said, firm and unequivocal, Zach nodding in agreement.

"Your father expects—"

"My father is not the ruler of my life," Keera snapped.

"Our instructions, Miss Miles, include ensuring you have the best medical treatment available," Hancock continued calmly. "The doctor advises further observation."

"You came very close to suffering heat stroke," the doctor added. "You could've done serious damage to your organs. Waiting one more day is wise."

She looked to Zach for support, but he gave her his best non-committal look, and she gave up.

"Okay, okay," she said, glaring at him. "But tomorrow's Monday. I have a class. Get me a phone so I can call and cancel."

Zach handed her his phone and took it back when she finished. "I've got calls to make myself. Boring reporter stuff—I'll deal with it in my room. Back soon."

An extra day in Flagstaff was a bonus—an extra day of safety. Also, time to dig up something on Vronsky. Maybe give the Russian more urgent problems than he thought he had.

He called a colleague in Chicago, a former staffer on a Russian-language newspaper.

"Vlad, it's Zach. Can you help me with something urgent?"

"Does it include beer and whiskey?"

"It will when I get back."

Zach gave him the names of the three Russians and sketchy descriptions.

"They're nasty types. You know any of them?"

"Can't say I do," Vlad replied. "The real nasty ones live in New York. Try Gennardy Sidirov. He freelances for the Russian press —crime beat. Acts like the mafia press office. They give him access, he writes puff pieces. Make that a top-shelf whiskey."

Sidirov was warm and sociable. "I'm not a fucking information bureau," he growled when Zach called with the three names. "Dig up your own stories."

"It's not a story. I'm helping a friend. But you could get a story out of it."

Sidirov relaxed—half a muscle.

"What kind of story?"

"One of them shafted the other."

"And?"

"Yuri Buteyko is in jail on a murder charge."

A pause.

"Where? Who put him there?"

"Flagstaff. A guy named Vronsky called the cops on him."

"You sure? Is this hearsay, or firsthand?" Sidirov was sounding like a real reporter now.

"The sheriff's office has a recording of Vronsky tipping them off. Yuri's lawyer can request it."

"How well do you know this Vronsky? Does he have top personal security?"

What was that? Was Sidirov asking if Vronsky was easy to kill? Jesus. Zach hadn't expected to be this close to a murder conspiracy.

"Maybe there's no story," Zach backpedaled. "Maybe I should check more first."

"You already gave me plenty," Sidirov said. "Others will follow up."

"What others?" But Zach already knew.

"Let's just say Buteyko's highly connected. You'd be smart to stay friendly on this one."

It dawned on Zach, crystal clear: Yuri's people would want revenge, no matter what Zach did. All he'd done was speed things along. It almost sounded... reasonable. He hoped Keera would see it that way.

"So," Sidirov asked, "does Vronsky have good security?"

"He carries more than just a phone in his pockets."

Sidirov laughed. "He'll need a lot more than that. Know where he is now?"

Zach hesitated. You can't make a deal with the devil without getting some soot on your soul.

"I believe he's heading to Chicago."

"You believe? I'm not a priest. I don't work in beliefs."

"He left Vegas yesterday, driving straight through. You can do the math."

"Do you know his exact destination?" Sidirov asked casually. Like it didn't matter at all.

This was the moment. Hand over Keera's address and Vronsky might disappear from their lives. But they'd be trading one danger for another. Most nightmares end when you wake up. This one would restart every morning.

"Yuri Buteyko knows it. He knows exactly where Vronsky wants to go."

"I'll call you. Maybe," Sidirov said, and hung up.

He hadn't asked what Zach's interest was—probably assumed he was just another bottom-feeder, clawing for scraps.

Zach sure felt like one.

Maybe that was the end of the whole rat-infested business.

Until he remembered the money.

Once Yuri told his people that Zach had control of Vronsky's cash—that poison pile of ransom profits—he would become a very desirable person to talk to.

By Monday morning, Keera still hadn't forgiven him for backing the doctor. She stayed silent as Hancock and Brooks drove them to the airport. All he'd done was help minimize a potential medical crisis, and she was pissed? Jesus.

They stopped at his motel. Zach threw his dirty clothes and the new ones into a laundry bag, took the elevator to the front desk.

"I need this," he said, holding up the bag. "Can I buy it?"

"That's so hard," the clerk said. "There's no procedure for this. I'll put it down as stolen and charge your card. How's that?"

"Sounds fair."

He wondered if his name would end up on Lovejoy's desk.

Probably not in the "too hard" basket.

Keera remained silent until Brooks pulled up to a Learjet.

Zach eyed the sleek fuselage.

"Daddy's?" he asked, his tone betraying his disdain.

"Yes, Zach. Let's not develop this topic right now, shall we?" Her face held warnings.

"Sure beats steerage class."

"Let's just go home. We can discuss the ways of the wealthy tomorrow."

"Your father smoothed the way. Got us out of a tight spot. Now he's flying us home. I feel like some school kid who messed up, and the adults are handling it. I hate that."

"Sometimes you just have to go along. We didn't have a lot of choice. I recall something similar happening to me yesterday."

She slipped her fingers into his. His frustration dissipated like steam.

Inside, the leather and wood trim offered the ambiance of a plush gentlemen's club. Zach settled into a broad lounge seat, pulling Keera down next to him. They sat close, hands linked. Brooks and Hancock took opposing seats at the front.

The stairs lifted, the jet surged forward. Seconds later, they were airborne.

When they leveled out, a flight attendant brought sandwiches and soft drinks. Zach asked for a beer.

She brought a Rolling Rock.

"Must be a mind reader like you," he said. "Haven't had one of these since college."

"I'm not a mind reader," Keera said.

"How long are the guards sticking around? What did you and your dad agree?"

"Nothing was agreed. If Dad gets his way, they'll stay with me forever." She frowned toward the front. "No chance they're moving in."

"So how do they watch you?"

"They'll park a van across the street. Work in shifts."

"Forever?"

"No. Dad will push me to move somewhere more secure. Like a whole floor in an apartment building. But I won't."

He squeezed her hand. There would never be a good time to tell her about Sidirov. About Vronsky likely living his last few hours. That it hadn't even been a difficult decision.

Keera broke the silence.

"You have a plan for Vronsky yet?"

She was definitely a mind reader.

"I called a contact. He was shocked about Yuri—said he's highly connected. Vronsky's in serious trouble."

He made it sound casual. She saw through it.

"You mean Yuri's people are going to kill Vronsky?"

"Who knows? Maybe he'll buy his way out."

"You're hoping he dies?"

"I'm hoping he falls into the arms of his enemies."

She stared at him. "You're not like them, but you're acting like them."

He let out a long breath.

"They were going to kill us, and you know it. Vronsky still might. I see no other way unless I find a gun and do it myself—which I wouldn't know how to."

"It's wrong."

Right, wrong—it didn't matter. The beasts were already out of the cage. A new thought surfaced.

"What did you mean about being saved from rape?"

She looked out the window.

"Semyon intended to rape me."

"While you're all fleeing to Vegas? He suddenly says, 'Stop the car, I want the woman now'?"

"Not exactly. I made them stop for a bathroom break."

"So—at the worst possible time—Semyon demands sex?"

"Not exactly."

"How exactly?"

She turned to him.

"I teased him. I knew if he reacted, Yuri would step in. I thought I could escape if they clashed. I didn't expect Yuri to shoot."

She'd played a dangerous game. The same game he was playing now.

"You set your enemies against each other, one of them died— and now you say I'm wrong?"

She had no answer. There was no answer. Moral certainties are for people who never have theirs tested.

She folded her hands in her lap. Was she accepting his logic— or praying for another way?

He let her think.

"What about your work?" she asked after a while. "Don't they want to know why you were in Arizona?"

She was changing the subject. Letting the debate drop—for now.

"Not yet. But it'll be a problem," he said. "*The Post* doesn't cover small-town murders. They'll want to know why I flew out here."

"Hmm. Tricky."

"Sure is. I can't mention the kidnapping or anything psychic, which means I can't explain why I was involved. I've got a great story—none of it publishable."

"So give back the expenses."

"Not that simple. If it looks like I faked the trip, I'm finished. Paying my own way makes it worse—makes it look premeditated. In my business, credibility is everything. Lose it, and I'm done."

"At least you won't suffer financially," she said. "You've got your millions."

He ignored the jab.

"This could be serious. Can you see my future in this?"

She leaned back in her seat.

"You've got problems."

CHAPTER 37

The company limo pulled away from the airport. Hancock and Brooks sat in the rear with them. All four stared silently out the windows.

Beside her, Zach tense enough to strangle himself, his palpable tension tangling her psychic senses. But he emanated one thing clearly: a spiky resolve not to back down in any confrontation with Vronsky. Images appeared, his earlier encounters with the Russians, his defeats, and she understood humiliation now drove him.

Hancock cleared his throat.

"There's a guard on your home, Miss Miles. He's been there since we got the call."

"So I can resume my life?" Keera asked.

"Not quite. We'll check the house first. Then you can collect any belongings while we secure the place."

"Where am I expected to stay?"

"Your father's arranged a hotel suite—used by diplomatic staff. Top-tier security. We'll escort you to any classes you need

242

to attend." He glanced at Zach. "We can accommodate Mr. Bones there too, if you wish."

"I get a bodyguard?" Zach asked. "That'll make my job tricky."

"You may dispense with our help if you prefer."

"Zach gets the same treatment as me," Keera said. "He put his life on the line to find me—and he came up with a way out."

Hancock waited for her to say more, but she stared him down. He turned back to the window. She caught a flash of his inner state: frustration, bewilderment—and something else. A foreboding. His life was about to break badly.

They turned onto her street and pulled up across from her house.

"Stay here," Hancock said. "We'll check everything. Then you can go in."

"Whatever. My spare keys are under the loose brick on the steps," she said.

"Under a brick?" Zach asked, peering out the window. "Couldn't find a better hiding spot? Like the mailbox?"

"We don't need them," Hancock said as he and Brooks exited. "We've already replaced the locks."

They crossed to a parked car. Hancock knocked on the driver's window. Knocked again. Bent low to look inside.

Then he straightened and yanked the handle. Locked.

Brooks drew his gun and smashed the side window with the butt.

The faint tinkle of shattering glass reached her ears—announcing what she already knew—horror had arrived.

The near-side limo door jerked open. She jumped.

Vronsky slid in, gun raised and aimed at Zach.

"No!" she cried. Bardo, you didn't warn me.

Vronsky rapped on the glass partition. It slid open. He showed the weapon to the startled driver.

"Face front. Both hands on the wheel."

The driver gripped the wheel like a lifebuoy.

Vronsky leaned to keep him in view. He'd ditched the leather jacket. Now wore a rumpled polo shirt. Unshaven. The whites of his eyes streaked red. His usual jollity replaced by something hard and grim.

"We need to talk, as you Americans say," he said, gun steady on Zach's chest.

"Thought our relationship was over," Zach said. "What else is there?"

"The money you took. I want it back—plus another two million. You've got twenty-four hours."

"Didn't you ask for money before? Resulted in four dead. You walked away with less than you started."

Don't argue, Zach. Just agree. Please.

"Last plan was messy," Vronsky said. "This one's simple. Send the money, I disappear. But if the money doesn't show, your girlfriend dies. You won't know how, or when, or who."

Keera saw Brooks with his head inside the guard's car. Hancock looked toward them, hesitated, but didn't spot Vronsky through the tinted glass.

He's in here, she screamed silently, but Hancock turned back.

"That's a tight deadline," Zach said, glancing at her.

She felt the rage in him—a living thing rising in his chest, whispering madness.

Outside, Brooks moved around Hancock, heading toward them, gun ready.

Don't walk—run!

"It's enough time," Vronsky said. "Money moves in seconds from your hands to mine. Touch it again, she dies."

"You don't get it," Zach said. "We know you. We knew about Sasha before you did. You threaten one of us, you force a response."

She saw his muscles bunch. No, Zach. Don't. Let him go.

Vronsky tensed at Sasha's name. "You have an informer. I'll find him and send you his body parts."

"If you get home."

Vronsky leaned closer. "There's only one equation: no money, no Miss Miles." He glanced outside. Brooks had stopped, waiting for a passing car.

"Twenty-four hours," Vronsky said. "After that, you'll know your future."

As he groped for the door handle behind him, Zach exploded —launched across the seat and slammed into him. They tumbled outside, grappling, Zach's hand on Vronsky's gun wrist pushing it down.

Keera flung her door open and screamed—raw, primal—a sound that snapped Brooks to life.

Vronsky chopped down on Zach's wrist and broke free. Cracked his head with the gun butt. Zach buckled. The Russian scrambled to his feet, and his face fractured. A gunshot split the air a nano second later, followed by a shriek, her shriek.

Vronsky's lower jaw disappeared. Another gunshot and the front of his shirt puckered wildly before blossoming red.

A bullet thwacked into the limo's bodywork.

He struggled to stay upright, grasping the door handle for support before slipping to the ground.

A man ran up. It wasn't Brooks.

A voice shouted, "Face down. On the ground!" Russian accent.

Hancock and Brooks dropped, still as corpses. The newcomer aimed a gun at them.

"Hands out front," he barked. They obeyed.

He kicked Brooks' weapon away.

The first man ignored Zach—still kneeling—rolled the body over and fired one last, unnecessary shot into Vronsky's skull.

He took two wallets from Vronsky's pants, and the gun, then walked off, his own gun down by his leg.

Seconds later, a car roared away behind them.

The execution had lasted sixty seconds.

Keera climbed out and pulled Zach to his feet. Held him close. Felt the tremor in his body, muscles like coiled wires. Tried to read him, but nothing came through.

Her own soul too shaken to receive.

She searched for Vronsky's spirit. Nothing. A plus. She wasn't ready for a psychic ambush.

Hancock and Brooks joined them, both with guns drawn— too late.

Hancock halted at the body. "Who was that guy?"

Zach spoke before she could. "The Russian that got away."

"Who were the others?"

"Hell if I know. Guess he pissed off more people than us."

His fingers probed his scalp. Blood. He wiped it on his jeans.

"Shit," Hancock muttered. "Okay, here's the story: You didn't know the guy, never saw him before. He jumped in, demanded money. You said no. He panicked, tried to run. Somebody else shot him. That's all you know. Got it?"

Vronsky dead less than a minute and Hancock already shaping the spin. Guys like him turned reality into fiction before breakfast.

"Got it," Zach said. "With that face, no one's matching him to those Flagstaff sketches."

He pulled Keera closer.

"Inside the house, you'll find vodka bottles and glasses in the living room."

Hancock nodded. Waiting for the bad news.

"Russian fingerprints all over them."

"Gotcha."

Those glasses would be spotless in an hour.

The driver, phone to ear, gave his location to someone. He turned to Hancock. "We stay. Police are coming." His voice was ragged, his face doomed. A man who'd just lost his job.

Keera understood. The security team had failed. Badly.

"I activated the LoJack immediately," he added, as if that helped.

"You did the right thing," she said. A vehicle tracker didn't stop a bullet. He didn't mention the unlocked doors. Didn't need to. The guilt was all over his face.

But Hancock and Brooks hadn't checked the street either. Vronsky had probably waited in a car for hours. They wouldn't last long in their roles.

"We need space," she said.

Before anyone objected, she led Zach across the street to her front steps.

"You've got blood in your hair." She pulled his head down.

"Clotting already. Not deep."

"Felt like a hammer." He pushed her hands away.

"I know. I felt it."

"My ancestors felt it." He paused, then changed the subject.

"Hancock will pitch this as a random robbery. Try to disconnect it from Sedona. If Vronsky stays unidentified, it stays manageable."

"Uh-huh." She barely took it in. Breathing deep, waiting for a sign, a whisper from Bardo.

Nothing.

Then something.

"He can't stay unidentified," she said.

"You know that? Or you think that?"

"He was fingerprinted entering the country. Still had fingers last I checked."

The image of Vronsky's ruined face made her stomach lurch.

Zach's head drooped. He swore softly.

"But it won't matter," she added.

He looked up, one eyebrow raised.

"When my father buries something, it stays buried. No one will follow it up."

"I hope you're right."

And then—Flint was with them.

"Wonderful to drop by," he said. "Beautiful outcome."

"Try living through it," she muttered. "Different experience."

"I said I was sorry, didn't I?"

"Yes. I'm just not in the mood. Near-death does that."

Flint spread his hands. "I did what I could to save y'all."

"Like what? Thought nice thoughts?"

"I tried to make amends. Did my best."

She gave him a brittle smile. "Flint, kindly fuck off to the white light and don't come back."

Sirens in the distance.

Zach sat motionless, sensing she was somewhere else.

"You seem tetchy," Flint said. "So I'll explain it simple."

She gave him the hurry-up glare.

"I saw Vronsky was going to be met by two guys. Don't know how—I just did."

She rolled her eyes.

"They didn't know he could drive so fast. Slept late. So I shouted at the first guy while he slept. Told him Vronsky was already there. He stirred, tossed, woke his pal. Said it came to him in a dream. They rushed over. Vronsky was already in the limo. Hell of a nail-biter."

She stared at him.

"I'm glad you were entertained. Bet you'd have enjoyed the lions eating Christians."

"Death's different now. Doesn't feel important. I'm dead, but not gone. Still part of the world."

"I'm not in the mood."

"You could thank me for saving your boyfriend."

"Thanks."

"I was hoping for something more fulsome."

"Ask for a medal at the Pearly Gates. If you get near them."

She wished him gone. He blinked.

"It's over," he said. "The Russians are done. You're free."

"And you're done here too?"

He raised a brow.

"You saying you'll miss me?"

"Definitely not. But I thank you for helping fix what you wrecked."

He faded.

She was left with Zach, another dead man, and questions no

one could answer.

CHAPTER 38

The police arrived in a herd of howling and lights. Some moved around the limo, unfurling crime scene tape. Others clustered around the guard's car below Zach and Keera, peering inside.

One officer straightened and said, "He's conscious."

Another siren announced an ambulance. The cops waved the medics over. They eased the guard out and stood him upright. Rivers of blood caked his face as he shuffled to the ambulance. Hancock followed. Another story to manage.

Zach stayed on the steps, his arm around Keera, both of hers around him.

A detective in a sports coat and jeans took statements from the guard and the limo driver. Then he approached.

"I'm Detective Norman Horn. Heard you folks had some trouble...?" His eyes landed on Zach and stayed there. "Did we speak last week? About a missing person?"

Zach nodded. "A simple misunderstanding, Detective. Miss Miles was meeting with a colleague when I thought she was supposed to be home. Thanks for asking—you were very under-standing that time." Sure, he was groveling, hoping Horn held no animosity. No reason to dig too deep.

"The same person who left without her handbag?"

This guy was going to pick at loose threads like a dog gnaw-ing a frayed couch.

"Women have many handbags, Detective." Zach managed a rueful grin.

Horn let his gaze drift to Keera, then back. "Is this the missing lady?"

Zach nodded. "We were reunited happily, soon after I spoke to you."

"And now you're both here, again, at a crime scene. Fascinat-ing."

"It shouldn't be. A gruesome coincidence, that's all."

"You ever worked in law enforcement?" Horn wasn't really asking. "Coincidences aren't as frequent as you think."

"So what connection would we have to a crazy mugger, other than being victims?"

Horn jotted something in his notebook. "What happened here? Give it to me from the moment you saw this guy."

Brooks stepped forward and placed a hand on Keera's shoul-der. "I represent Mr. Bones and Miss Miles," he said. "I'd like to confer with my clients before any statement is made."

"I'm sure you would," Horn said, eyeing Brooks' suit.

"We'd also like to leave," Brooks continued. "Staying here is very distressing for them."

"I didn't hear you ask how they feel. How do you know?"

"We'd just exited the limo when the mugging occurred. I can confidently assume the state of their feelings."

Brooks turned to Zach, "Are you distressed?"

"Extremely. It's been a horrifying nightmare—to be held up at gunpoint and witness a random killing like that. We want out of here."

Brooks asked Keera. "You've just lived through an appalling experience, haven't you?"

She nodded. "I'll never forget it."

A television van pulled up. The crew spilled out—camera operators finding their angles, a sound guy uncoiling cords, a leggy blonde reporter adjusting her hair in a mirror.

Horn looked back to Zach. "Unpleasant business, I know. But we just want a brief statement for now. If we argue, we'll be here till sunrise."

Brooks looked ready to protest, then thought better of it.

"The victim," Horn said, glancing at the limo, "I don't need forensics to tell me those are soft-nosed bullets. Someone wanted to make sure he didn't survive." He turned back to Zach. "Start from the top. Did you know the deceased?"

"No," Zach said. That one word—one lie—could cost him everything if Horn chose to dig. "We were getting out of the limo when he jumped in and demanded money. Must've thought we were loaded. I got angry and stupid and tackled him. Then these other guys came out of nowhere and he went down. It was horrible."

"You see the killers?"

"Not really. I was pretty woozy after he hit me with his gun."

Zach touched his head. Horn leaned over and inspected the wound.

"It's a scratch. Bleeding's stopped."

"Glad something's going right."

Horn jotted more notes. "Sounds like this guy stepped on someone else's turf. The killing might be unrelated to your mugging. Maybe that poor guy in the guard's car was another mugging target."

He turned to Keera. "Can you add anything?"

"Yes," she said. "He told the driver to face the front and keep his hands on the wheel."

The news crew edged closer, cops struggling to hold them back.

Horn turned to Zach again. "Name?"

"Zachary Bones."

"Right. Bones." Locking it in. "You can go for now. Leave your ID details with the sergeant. Report to the precinct tomorrow at ten for full statements."

"We'll be there," Brooks said, ushering them away.

Zach glanced at Vronsky's body, now covered by a blue groundsheet.

Hancock and Brooks whistled down a cab and got them moving. Keera looked back at the bloodied guard.

"Is he a friend of yours?" she asked Hancock.

"Not a friend, but one of us. Stand-up guy, knows the protocol. He'll say he was caught by surprise when he got mugged. No connection to you two."

The protocol. A weasel word for a heap of lies.

And the police? They had to be the dumbest bunch around if they didn't wonder about two muggings, twenty yards apart, both linked.

"What did the Russian say that got you fighting mad?" Hancock asked Zach.

"He wanted six million in twenty-four hours or we'd both die."

Hancock digested this. "You get all testy because of the amount or is jumping armed guys your usual habit?"

"Usually I wait till they're squeezing the trigger. The closer to death, the more fun."

Keera cut in. "The unlocked doors caused all the problems."

No answer to that. Hancock dropped the issue.

"We'll skip your place. Straight to the secure location."

"And my clothes?" Keera asked. "And materials for class?"

"List them. I'll have everything you need tonight. We've already sent over a selection of your wardrobe."

"You touched my clothes?"

Hancock looked uncomfortable. "No choice. Anything else, you can buy tomorrow. Use my corporate card."

"Bring my handbag. It's on the coffee table."

"Of course." He nodded, clearly not looking for a fight. He'd lost his authority—and he knew it.

When my father hears about all this, you'll both be out, she thought, but didn't say it.

To Zach Hancock added, "We found a few of your things too. All at the hotel."

Zach didn't answer.

She glanced at him. His face was blank, but she knew what he was thinking. It had taken months for her to let him keep clothes at hers. Now all of them were gone.

The hotel suite was nearly a penthouse—her father's idea. Extravagant, but he knew she'd object.

A security guard outside the door looked like he could hold off an army. Hancock told him, "Say hello and goodnight to Miss

Miles."

The guard nodded. "Goodnight, Miss Miles."

"He's the only voice you can trust," Hancock said. "Don't open the door unless it's him."

"Or you," she added, knowing she'd never see him again.

"Of course. I'll be back at ten a.m. Good night."

Zach collapsed on the couch. "I'm just gonna let my stomach uncurl."

She settled onto his lap, kissed him. "It's over. I'm sure of it."

"We should celebrate, huh?"

He sounded like he'd rather wallow. She kissed him again. He didn't respond. She stood. "I'm going to shower and change. Then we'll have a special dinner sent up. I expect an interesting partner."

"Yeah, sure," he said. Didn't move.

She wasn't surprised. Aftershock. He'd seen his own death in Vronsky's. But he'd get through it.

She was drying her hair when Bardo appeared in the mirror, perched on the tub's edge.

"Oh, you," she said. "There's more?"

"You look crisp as a new morning."

"Thanks." She waited.

"It's all over, apart from..." He nodded toward the main room.

"He's making a decision."

"About what?"

"He'll tell you. Accept it. Don't assert your viewpoint. You need healing."

"You're telling me how to live now? You said the future was mine to shape."

"It is. But I'm also here to help."

He shimmered and vanished.

She came out to find Zach opening champagne. A trolley held covered dishes.

"You spoken to your guide lately?" he asked, easing the cork.

"This thing over yet?"

"Pretty much. Just confirmed."

"He told you that? Where was he when we almost got killed?"

"He's always around. Mostly, I have to figure things out."

"He'd let you die? I don't believe it."

"There are worse things than death, Zach."

"Didn't feel that way with a gun in my face."

He was easing out of shock, wrapping it into a narrative he could live with.

"Let it go," she said. "You'll go mad chasing what-ifs."

"You're right." He gave her a look. "You said my expenses would be a problem?"

"Nothing major. I saw frowns, suspicion—but they don't want to lose you. It'll be dropped."

"You could've told me. I've been worrying for days."

"You were annoying at the time." She smiled sweetly.

He considered her confession. Decided to move on. "I bet our statements will be taken at face value. That detective lost interest fast."

"Same here. You're getting psychic?"

"Not in my lifetime."

"By the way, one of the gunmen removed two wallets from Vronsky's pants pocket.

He lifted his head. 'What?"

"Didn't they remove yours when they jumped you in the motel?"

"Dammit. Those killers now have my ID."

Keera said, "It could be a problem in the future, but it would be far worse for us if the cops had found your ID on Vronsky."

He took it in. "Let's hope you're right."

"Let's worry about the future when it arrives. We're done for now."

He filled two flutes, handed her one. They touched them together, no words required, and drank.

She leaned back on the doorframe. "Been meaning to ask—doesn't it kill you not being able to spend that money?"

"Not really. It won't be mine for long."

"Meaning?"

"I'm giving it away. To Yuri's people."

"That was part of the deal?"

"No. But they'll come for it anyway. You suggested buying off Vronsky. This is better—buy the rest of them off. Yuri will tell them."

His logic was solid, if distasteful. Probably the only move they had to end this nightmare. That's why Bardo had asked her not to challenge Zach's decision.

She said. "You're right, it's the only way."

As if he hadn't heard, he continued. "They'll come after it, one of us will die, maybe both of us. We'll be torn apart whatever happens."

He stared into his glass, searched for more words. Came up with the right ones. "I'd lose you. I don't ever want to lose you."

She eased off the doorframe.

"Come over here and say that."

THE END

THE END

ACKNOWLEDGEMENT

As always in the process of fiction creation, there are others who labor to make the author appear better than he thought he was.

My thanks go to Abigail Nathan for an early, surgical overview that helped shape my first ideas.

Also to Arlene Robinson, who edited subsequent drafts, and showed me how much I still had to learn.

Thanks to the NSW Writers' Centre for the use of their facilities and the Open Genre critique group for a year's worth of comments. In particular I want to acknowledge the constant advice given by Brian Bell, Charles Cox, Helen Lyne, Lucy Stevens, Alita Tanswell, and Suzanne Tindal.

I'd also like to thank my fellow scribblers in Los Angeles: Carrie Christensen, Suzanne Park and Leslie Ferguson, for gleefully pointing out clunky sentences, arguing for comprehensible grammar over stylish outpourings, but most of all for getting involved in the story and demanding improvements.

Thanks to Anita Saunders for the final proofing.

ABOUT THE AUTHOR

Parker Rimes

Parker Rimes has spent his life in Europe, Australia, the UK and the US. When not writing, he likes to read four or five books a week. Some of them he completes.

In the course of his journalist life, he interviewed over a thousand people who claimed paranormal experiences occurred in their homes. Many of these stories seemed truthful, and inspired his career as a fiction author.

Diligent research for his novels led him to enroll in a school for mediums, where he failed nearly every psychic test. But he can now predict where to find a good parking space slightly better than the average person.

His favorite pastime is discovering new verbs, and wishing he'd thought of them first.

He likes animals but prefers that most of them stay in their own home. His favorite wines are those sold close to wherever he lives.

You can find his latest musings here:
Www.parkerrimes.com

BOOKS BY THIS AUTHOR

The Backward Time Traveler

A psychic receives an impossible task: to travel back 200 years and rescue a sacred stone from a Sioux tribe. She's persuaded take along a pesky reporter, but he's more interested in her body than her so-called mission. Great.

Inserted secretly into a band of Indians, they struggle to adapt their city ways to a more brutal lifestyle. Their situation abruptly worsens after a savage Crow attack. Even more shocking is the revelation that the door to the past can't be closed once it's forced open.

Never Show Them Money

When too much money is not nearly enough. Zach Bones, a reporter on the Chicago Post, has liberated three million dollars from a Russian kidnappers' bank account. Now he's offering the money to a rival syndicate in grateful payment for them eliminating his psychic girlfriend's kidnappers.

Trouble is, these Russians believe that if he took money out of one bank account, he could do it again. For them. And forever.

The Darker You Get

Reporter Zach Bones still has Russian mob money. He'd like to keep it; his psychic girlfriend Keera says give it away—it's dirty. A hitman Lev wants it also and uses a sniper rifle to make his point. The cops can't understand why a hitman would target an ordinary reporter, and grow suspicious of Zach's lack of explanation.

He can't find a solution that leaves him with a life worth living. And Keera's abilities can only do so much to protect both of them. Especially when Lev is steadily losing his grip on reality.

Eye Of The Beholder

Zia checks out a dating website. It lets her view her prospective soulmate's world through his eyes. She sees blue skies. Leafy trees. A car interior. And a pair of feet—chained together. Puzzled and concerned, Zia searches for the truth in the glossy world of people-matching, and uncovers disturbing surgical procedures.

Worse, her bestie is involved...

Catch Your Death

There's weird, and there's seriously weird. One of them can really wreck a girl's evening. And every evening after that.

Reporter Ruby Moskewitz is interviewing a famous Professor of Biology when he vanishes during a meal break. Just like that. Has this anything to do with his new drug that accelerates brain?

When she contacts his university she's told the professor has a contagious condition and had to be isolated urgently. This is a lie, she knows it, and she investigates.

Her one advantage? She's in sole possession of the drug that gifts normal people with abnormal powers.

The Art Of Dash

When Chicago journalist Zach Bones incriminates a major drug dealer Jason Virgil, he discovers he's been set up. Virgil is killed in jail on the orders of his rival Frankie Ritchie, and Zach's now a suspect. Worse, the dead and wrathful Virgil begins to extract revenge on everybody involved.

Zach's psychic girlfriend Keera can save him, she thinks. But after Virgil murders his killer by psychic attack, she realizes that no human can stop him.